Siren Sisters

DANA LANGER

Aladdin

New York   London   Toronto   Sydney   New Delhi

ALADDIN

An imprint of Simon & Schuster Children's Publishing Division
1230 Avenue of the Americas, New York, New York 10020
First Aladdin hardcover edition January 2017
Text copyright © 2017 by Dana Langer
Jacket illustration copyright © 2017 by Hari & Deepti
For information about special discounts for bulk purchases, please contact
Simon & Schuster Special Sales at 1-866-506-1949 or business@simonandschuster.com.
The Simon & Schuster Speakers Bureau can bring authors to your live event.
For more information or to book an event contact the Simon & Schuster Speakers
Bureau at 1-866-248-3049 or visit our website at www.simonspeakers.com.
Jacket designed by Jessica Handelman
Interior designed by Michael Rosamilia
The text of this book was set in Mrs Eaves.
Manufactured in the United States of America 1216 FFG
2 4 6 8 10 9 7 5 3 1
Library of Congress Cataloging-in-Publication Data
Names: Langer, Dana, author.
Title: Siren Sisters / by Dana Langer.
Description: First Aladdin hardcover edition. | New York : Aladdin, 2017. |
Summary: "Lolly Salt's three sisters are sirens—young woman who lure ships to their doom.
And as Lolly's 13th birthday approaches she's about to become one too. But when it
becomes clear that someone in town knows the Salt girls' secret, Lolly sets out to learn
how this happened to her family and if she can prevent it."—Provided by publisher.
Identifiers: LCCN 2016000134 | ISBN 9781481466868 (hc) | ISBN 9781481466882 (eBook)
Subjects: | CYAC: Sirens (Mythology)—Fiction. | Supernatural—Fiction. |
Sisters—Fiction. | Families—Fiction. | Maine—Fiction.
Classification: LCC PZ7.1.L344 Si 2017 | DDC [Fic]—dc23
LC record available at https://lccn.loc.gov/2016000134

for M.

Chapter 1

The siren sings so sweetly that she
lulls the mariners to sleep.
—*Leonardo da Vinci*

Now that I know the truth, I sometimes picture my sisters in headlights, the way they would have looked on that cold February night, armed with shovels and pickaxes, and digging in the graveyard. They have Dad's truck running, parked on the dirt road, and ropes they stole from a fishing boat. They're wearing snow boots and Dad's old work gloves, and they're struggling not to slip on the ice.

Of course, that's how I see it in my imagination. Like most of our family stories, I don't know all the facts and details. It's the curse of the youngest sibling. I mean, maybe there weren't any shovels. Maybe there was a backhoe or something. And maybe they didn't leave the truck running and the headlights on. Maybe they had lanterns. But this is what I do know: They must have been terrified out there in the darkness, afraid of what they would find and afraid it wouldn't work, that they'd put their lives in the hands of a vengeful sea witch for nothing. And also this: The three of them were the prettiest grave robbers in history. That I know for sure.

One week earlier

This is how it happens: We reach the cliffs at dawn, in the middle of an electrical storm. Lightning splits the sky, and a strange, wild wind howls through the trees and tangles our hair. We walk right up to the edge, where we can see the waves breaking on the rocks below, and my sisters hold hands and begin to sing. Their voices are pure and perfect, and their song is so sweet you can practically taste it; it's the musical equivalent of strawberry lemonade on a hot summer day.

I can't sing like they can. Not yet, anyway. I try to join them, but every time I open my mouth, instead of that beautiful strawberry sound, it's like the croaking of a frog. The musical equivalent of a lump of mashed potatoes. And so I just stand there in the rain and mouth the words.

Out on the water, a cargo ship, a massive freighter stacked about twenty feet high, heads for shore. My sisters sing louder, and I cover my eyes with my hands and peek through my fingers. I want to be brave like they are. I want to act like I don't care. But in case you don't already know, a shipwreck is a terrible thing to see. There's a tremendous crash, the sound of metal scraping against rock, and then an awful groaning as the entire ship tilts and breaks apart. Cables snap, and cargo containers slide from the deck and fall into the ocean like cannonballs. The crew can't do anything but abandon their vessel and await rescue.

The whole process is exhausting, and we fall asleep right there in the grass, Lara, Lula, Lily, and me, lying in a tangled heap of bodies and wet clothes. In the morning, the sun comes out, and we trudge sleepily back home, squinting, sweat trickling down our backs. Sometimes a truck pulls over and the driver offers us a ride. They're usually fishermen on their way to market, hauling huge barrels filled with silvery-black sea bass and mussels and lobsters. They think we're just normal girls, and we play along. *Just out for a walk,* we explain. *Beautiful morning. Thank you so much; we'd love a ride.*

Our family owns the Starbridge Diner, home of the best blueberry pie and bottomless cup of coffee in northern New England, and my sisters are known as the best waitresses in Starbridge Cove. They can tell what you want to order just by looking at you. They know if you want a cheeseburger, and they know how you want it cooked, and don't even bother pretending to be interested in the fruit salad; they already know that what you *really* want is a vanilla milk shake and a slice of pie. And they'll bring it to you, whether you ask for it or not.

We're all there on Sunday afternoon when the local news comes on the radio: *"Another disastrous shipwreck this morning, just north of Bergstrom Marina . . ."*

I stop rolling silverware in napkins and glance at my sisters, but they don't make eye contact. They play it cool.

"Rain's stopping," Lula says. "I'm going to get the door." She turns the dial on the radio, and it switches to the local folk rock station, playing one of our dad's new songs. Then she crosses the room, red rubber sandals smacking against her feet, and flips the sign from CLOSED to OPEN.

"Lula!" Lara pokes her head out from the kitchen. "Are you wearing flip-flops?"

"Yeah, I'm gonna change in a second."

"Now please! And, Lily, take off those sunglasses. Let's try to be a little professional here."

The screen door slams and Dad comes into the kitchen. "Hey, Lolly."

I wave to him through the window between the kitchen and the counter. "How was practice?"

"Fine." He stomps his boots on the mat, hangs his faded green army jacket on the coatrack, and sets his guitar case, covered in antiwar stickers and peace signs, down in the corner.

I jerk my thumb toward the radio. "I like the new song. Are you playing it for the festival?"

"Yup." He slips an apron over his head and goes to turn on the stove. "The exciting live debut of 'On the Ghost Road.' Busy afternoon?"

I shake my head and turn back to my napkin rolls. "No, it was super quiet because of the storm. We decided to close for a little while."

"Well, that's probably for the best. Tourists don't come out during weather like that. You girls get stuck in it?"

"No. We were fine."

"Good." Dad bends down and kicks a mouse-trap back under the sink. "Glad to hear it."

I hop down off my stool and busy myself setting tables.

Next week, when I turn thirteen, I'll be allowed to work as a waitress like the others. For now, I still have to do the menial tasks, carrying and cleaning, and showing people to their seats.

At five o'clock I have a break for dinner, and Jason will come to visit. I cut slices of our favorite pies, apple crumb for him and wild blueberry for me, and then I grab my jacket and a mug of black coffee and wait by the door.

Lula leans over the counter, licking key lime

pie filling off the edge of a spatula. "What are you doing, Lolly? Waiting for your boyfriend?" She and Lily start laughing.

"Lula, get that out of your mouth!" Lara comes around the counter and nudges me with her hip. "What's wrong, little lady?" Lara has this amazing gift for taking the lamest expression and making it sound cool. She makes you wish you'd thought of saying it first. Only then it wouldn't have sounded cool; it would have just been lame.

I blow on my coffee. "He's not my boyfriend."

"Sure," Lily says. "That's why you're turning bright red."

"Oh, quiet!" Lara shushes her. "She's always turning bright red. She can't help that." She takes a pencil from her apron pocket and starts twisting my ponytail up into a knot. Lara is a master of effortless hairstyles that look messy in the perfect way. "You go and have a nice time, Lolly." She sticks the pencil through my hair just as the door opens and Jason comes in, water dripping from his bright blue raincoat. He's kind of small for his age and really skinny, and he can't help staring at my sisters. Nobody can.

"Come on!" I grab his arm and pull him back toward the door.

Lara lifts two fingers in the air. "Peace out, Girl Scout!"

The picnic tables are located beneath a circle of pine trees, and the benches are still wet from the morning's storm, but we take our napkins and dry a space for ourselves. Jason has to wipe the bench exactly ten times before he'll sit down, even though we both know it's perfectly clean. While he's doing that, I open the pastry boxes and take a sip of my coffee.

"How can you drink that stuff, Lolly?"

"Coffee? I don't know . . . it helps me stay awake."

"Yeah, but why are you always so tired in the first place?"

"You want to try some?"

He makes a face. "No way. I don't even like the smell."

I shrug and take another sip. "Coach Bouchard and Nurse Claire are definitely dating. I'm, like, ninety percent sure."

"So what?"

"So it's totally weird. I mean, they're both school employees."

Jason picks up his fork. "How does this affect you in any way?"

"I saw them in the parking lot yesterday. Holding hands!"

He takes a bite of apple crumb and chews thoughtfully. "Still doesn't answer my question."

"I just don't like seeing people where they're not supposed to be. I mean, they're in charge of us at school. I don't want to think about them having, like, *lives*. You know?"

"I guess."

"Oh!" I set the mug down, splashing coffee everywhere. "Okay, I almost forgot. I have something really exciting to tell you!"

Jason glances at me and then unfolds his napkin and starts wiping up the spill. "More exciting than this?"

At school, we're learning about inverse proportions, and sometimes I think you could map my friendship with Jason on one of those triangular diagrams. The more excited I am about something, the exponentially more skeptical he becomes. "That new giant squid documentary is playing at the aquarium, the one you're always telling me about. I saw it in the paper."

"*Mysteries of the Deep*? I already knew about that."

"Oh. Well, this is a special showing. Four p.m., and kids go for free. Plus, they give you a free soda. We can take the bus right after school."

"Are we still kids?"

"It says anyone under fifteen."

"Well, I'd like to go, but I actually, um, I have something to do."

"Something to do? You've been talking about this documentary for months. What do you have to do?"

Jason takes a deep breath and pushes away his pie. He has copper-colored hair and freckles, and, just like me, he turns bright red when he's nervous. Which is clearly now.

"Jason, what is it?"

He takes a crumpled flyer from his pocket and smooths it down on the table.

ANNUAL HALLOWEEN REGATTA!

SPONSORED BY BISHOP'S FISH

AGE 10 AND UP

OCTOBER 31ST

BERGSTROM MARINA

Suddenly I'm not in the mood for pie either. "Why do you have that?"

He looks at me. "Because I want to sign up. And tryouts are tomorrow."

"But you get seasick. I mean, you hate sailing."

"I hate my stepbrothers," he corrects. "And I hate their boat. That doesn't mean I hate sailing."

Part of the reason Jason and I are such good friends is because we both know what it's like to be the youngest in the family and the worst at everything. In Jason's case, it's sailing. His stepdad is a developer who owns practically every commercial property in town. He owns the entire marina, plus a condo complex, four motels, and two boats. Jason has three stepbrothers, all tall and strong like their dad, and they all sail competitively. For a while, they dragged Jason along on the boat too, but while everyone else was out frolicking on the bow in bathing suits, sipping champagne and eating fancy cheese, Jason would spend the afternoon with his hood pulled up and his head in his arms. Finally, during their last outing, he threw up all over the deck, and now he's allowed to just stay home.

"Anyway," he continues, "sailing is big at Starbridge Prep. I need to start practicing."

"But that's still a year away."

"So?"

"So I think this is a terrible idea."

"Why?"

"Because . . . well, what if something bad happens?"

"Like what?"

"Like, what if you get hurt? What if you get seasick again? What if you fall in the water and get eaten by a shark? Or a giant squid!"

"Are you kidding?"

"And what about *Mysteries of the Deep*? It's our last chance to see it. I mean, you said yourself it's a groundbreaking film, something every aspiring marine biologist should see on the big screen."

Jason stands and shoves the flyer back in his

pocket. "You're being so weird right now, Lolly."

"What do you mean? Where are you going?"

He shakes his head. "I'm not hungry anymore."

He climbs over the bench and squelches away through the muddy grass, leaving me alone with our half-eaten pie. Of course, it's not really about the documentary. I mean, a person doesn't get to be best friends with Jason O'Malley for ten years without watching about eight million marine biology documentaries, and let's face it, once you've seen one giant squid, you've pretty much seen them all. There's something more serious at stake here. If Jason joins that sailing competition, or any sailing competition, his life could be in danger. And my sisters and I are the reason.

That night I can't sleep. I toss and turn and stare out my open window, waiting for signs of a storm. Finally, I throw back my blankets, flick on a flashlight, and pull out a stack of contraband library books from underneath my bed. Research. For the last month I've been secretly searching the school library for information about sirens, hoping I might discover an explanation for what's happening to me and, more important, how to stop it. Mrs. Anderson, the school librarian, rules the stacks with an iron hand, but I've figured out how to slide my bag down the counter behind the book scanner when she's not looking so it won't set off the alarm. I'm very thorough and organized with my research, more than I ever am with my real schoolwork. I read all the books, I read all the footnotes, and then I read all the books referenced in the footnotes. I highlight important information, and I write down important quotations when I want to remember the author's own words. I've found a lot of fascinating facts about sirens from all over the world this way. Mami Wata of Africa with her braided black hair and snakes coiled over her shoulders and waist. The murderous *rusalki* of Russia with their green eyes and translucent skin. But most of these scholars don't believe in the existence of sirens, let alone begin to understand them on any practical level. Basically, there's not much useful information for a real-life siren-in-training like me, especially not when it comes to being a siren in middle school in a tiny town in Maine that's not really known for anything except folk music and seafood. That's why I started keeping my own journal, a field guide of sorts.

*SOME THINGS ABOUT SEVENTH GRADE THAT
MAKE IT DIFFICULT TO BE A SIREN:*

*School starts at 8 a.m., and you have to show up on
time and stay awake for algebra, even if you were up
causing shipwrecks until 4 a.m. the night before.*
*You have to change into sneakers for gym class, and
there is a good chance that everyone in the locker
room will see the scales on your feet.*
*The boy you like may decide to join the sailing team, and
then you'll be in the awkward position of having to
lure him to his doom.*

After a while, I close my books and tiptoe down the hall to Lara's room. I crawl in next to her amid the heaps of clothing and magazines she leaves scattered everywhere.

"Lara," I whisper. She smells like our mom used to—like clean laundry and sea spray. She used to have hair like our mom's too, thick and straight and midnight black, but of course that changed when she became a siren and the Sea Witch turned her hair the color of butter.

"Mmmm?" She's still half-asleep.

"I don't want to do this anymore. I'm scared."

She rolls over and drapes one arm over me. "You have to, Lolly. You're almost thirteen."

"But why?"

"I'll explain it when you're older."

I'm finally starting to fall asleep, when I hear the sound of the wind chimes ringing and the rusty old weather vane creaking on the roof. I pull the blankets up over my head, but then the whole room lights up, and a sound like a drum rattles the windows and shakes the walls. Lara pushes the covers back. "Come on, Lolly," she says. "She's calling."

In the morning, Lula and Lily wake us both by jumping on the bed. Lara takes her pillow and swats at them, but they just jump higher.

"We made coffee!"

Lula lands on top of me, giggling, and her necklace brushes against my face. We all have the same one, a heart-shaped locket that Lara had made for us after our mom died, and we wear them every day. "Wake up, little one!" Her sun-streaked hair is in a high side ponytail, and she's wearing a T-shirt that says: CALL ME.

Everyone stops jumping, and we huddle together with the blankets pulled around our shoulders. Lula distributes the steaming mugs of coffee they've left on the nightstand, and Lara starts braiding Lily's hair.

It's September, and the mornings are already getting cold. We live in an old farmhouse at the edge of town, about half a mile from the diner, and you can always feel a draft through the glass windowpanes and the gaps in the thin shingle walls.

"Ow!" Lula complains. "Someone's feet are freezing!"

"Probably Lolly's." Lara smiles at me. "She sleeps with me most nights, and it's like being in bed with a little brick of ice."

"I dreamed about Mom again," Lula says. "She was playing her guitar in the middle of the river."

"You did?" I sit up a little higher on the pillows. "What else? How did she look? Did she say anything about me?"

"We have to go, guys." Lily swings her long, skinny legs over the side of the bed. "Come on. We're gonna be late again."

I bury my face in the steam from the coffee and breathe it in. The mugs are as big as bowls and filled right to the brim. "I'm still so tired."

"We slept about four hours," Lara consoles me. "You'll get used to being up all night. It's just that you're still growing."

I sigh into my coffee. "I hate it."

"Why?" Lula asks. "It's amazing."

"Yeah," Lily echoes. "Do you have some kind of *problem* with being powerful and immortal and irresistible?"

"I have a problem with never getting any sleep. Besides, I think I was stronger and more powerful when I was doing gymnastics. Remember when I dislocated my elbow falling off the balance beam and didn't even cry?"

"Yes," Lily says. "How could we forget? You tell that story, like, every day."

I slide my hand over the now-healed elbow, which still hurts sometimes when it's cold out or about to rain. "I really miss it."

"Well, I don't see how. Every time I turn around you're upside down or doing cartwheels."

"I found her hanging in the coat closet last week," Lula reports. "She's like a bat."

"That's not the same. I don't understand why. I mean, don't you sometimes just want to be normal?"

They all exchange glances and then Lily sighs dramatically. "Whatever. You're just jealous because you can't do it yet. You can't sing like we can."

"Oh, come on," Lara says. "You don't have to be so mean about it. She's still just a child."

"I'm not a child!" As I say the words, I'm aware of how childish I sound. Well, too late. I climb out of bed and stomp into the bathroom to brush my teeth. I turn on the tap, but I can still hear them talking about me over the rush of water. They want me to grow up. They're tired of me being "so sensitive and immature," always whining about being tired or cold or having to quit gymnastics.

The first time I said I felt sad about a ship we'd wrecked, Lily just rolled her eyes. "You don't get it, Lolly."

"So explain it to me."

"Don't be a loser."

"I'm not a loser. I just feel bad."

"Well, that pretty much makes you a loser."

There was a time when Lily and I were like mirrors of each other. We were both born during freak snowstorms in September, only one year apart, and people always thought we were twins. Sometimes, we'd pretend it was true. We'd dress alike and sleep in the same bed and speak to each other in a language that no one else could understand.

But Lily started having problems after our mom died, and she had to meet with a lot of doctors and take a lot of tests. Anyway, it turned out she's actually some sort of genius, and they decided to move her up to ninth grade. She got to become a siren, a waitress, and a high school student all in the same year, and now it's like she's determined to prove she's worthy of all that maturity, which seems to involve being really mean all the time and acting like she barely knows me.

I wait a few minutes until I'm sure they've gone, and then I braid my hair, splash water on my face, and head downstairs. I pull a ripped wool sweater on over the leggings and T-shirt I slept in the

night before, and I shove my feet into an old pair
of rain boots that are too big for me. Our closets
are all in tangles, and it's impossible to tell who
anything belongs to. I think this sweater was my
mom's. I think the boots are Lily's.

Lily is already in the truck, and leaning on the
horn.

Lula puts on a denim jacket and pulls her long
hair free from the collar. She grabs an armload of
textbooks and rushes out the door.

Lara is still pouring her coffee into a thermos.
She gives me a quick, worried smile as she reaches
for her keys. "Your hair's starting to change." She
tugs on my braid.

"What do you mean?"

"Just that it's starting to get lighter, you know,
like ours."

"Does it look really weird?"

"Well, we can always bleach it for you, but it
might be better just to let it grow in naturally. It's
sort of a pretty color."

"I liked it the way it was."

Lily leans on the horn again, and Lara gives me
another crooked smile. "All set?"

I nod and sling my schoolbag, a slouchy, multi-colored tote bag I found in the attic last summer, over my shoulder. "All set."

On my way out the door, I catch sight of my reflection in the hall mirror. The glass is all smoky and warped, but still, I can see it. My hair is mostly dark, the way it's always been, but the platinum is creeping in from the ends. It's a bright, bleached, electric-looking shade, and I can begin to see her then, my full siren self. She's just a little taller than I am now, and she has hair the color of lightning.

Chapter 2

Their song, though irresistibly
sweet, was no less sad . . .
—*Walter Copland Perry*

We all attend Sunrise County Public Schools, which is a conglomeration of five regional schools, and Lara drives us there, smushed like sardines, in Dad's old pickup truck. The truck always smells like smoke and peppermint and isn't meant to have more than three passengers, so I sit half on Lula's lap. My sisters are all in high school now, but I just started middle school, so they have to drop me off first. On our way, Lily turns on the radio, and they all start singing along. They harmonize with each other so well, it's like they share a brain. I just sit there and look out the window.

We pass the library, the elementary school, and the village green. And then we pass the new grave-yard and I hold my breath.

The new graveyard is located in the center of town, near the town hall and the Presbyterian church. It's surrounded by a wrought iron fence and full of trimmed hedges and big gleaming tombstones. It is a very nice cemetery. Still, we prefer the old graveyard.

The old graveyard is set back in the forest on a hill, and most of the gravestones are crumbling and half-broken, irregular and misshapen like a set of crooked teeth. Our mother, especially, thought it was beautiful. "All those poor exiled souls," she used to say. "The witches and wander-ers. Unwelcome, even in death." She'd take us there and play her guitar sometimes, and we'd lie in the grass and my sisters would sing, and we'd eat the wild strawberries that grew up between the gaps in the stone wall. Since she died, though, we haven't been back there at all.

We pull up outside the main entrance of the

school, and Lula tilts the rearview mirror to
apply her lipstick. I swing the passenger door
open wide, and Lara passes me my bag. "Do you
have everything?"

"I think so. My stomach sort of hurts."

"You'll be fine."

"I wish I was going with you guys."

Lula grabs my hand. "Make a fist!" I do, and
she uses her lipstick to draw a bright pink heart on
the top of my hand.

"What are you doing?"

"So you can keep us with you all the time," she
says. "So you won't be afraid."

I slide down from the truck and wave to them.
"Have a good day!"

They beep the horn a few times to say good-
bye, and then they pull away.

Without my sisters around, I always feel a lot
smaller. Or maybe it's just that the world seems a
lot bigger. I shoulder my bag and climb the front
steps, and then I push open the heavy double
doors and hurry inside. I'm definitely late.

After the bell rings, the main hallway at school
transforms into the loneliest place in the world.

It's like being on Mars. All of the classroom doors are already shut, and a sea of checkerboard floor stretches before me. It's so quiet that I can hear the fluorescent lights buzzing, and the ticking of the clock on the wall. 8:20. It's only the fourth week of school and I've already been late seven times.

I hurry past the big corkboard that announces important events, including the upcoming folk festival and sailing tryouts, and that features a picture of the school's mascot, the Lobster, beneath the school's slogan: SUNRISE MIDDLE SCHOOL— EXPLORING NEW DEPTHS!

Each spring, Sunrise Middle School hosts its annual Lobsterfest fund-raiser, and all of the eighth graders dress up in bright red lobster suits and serve people corn on the cob. You'd think at Lobsterfest people would notice that a red lobster is a cooked lobster and realize it shouldn't be smiling or serving anybody corn, but if they do, they don't seem to mind. As our dad always says, reality isn't nearly as important in this town as tradition.

I hook a right at the water fountain, and I try to run in Lily's too-big rubber boots without making too much noise or tripping over my bag. Still, just as I'm about to reach the doorway of my classroom, the boots get the better of me, and the bag swings forward around my waist and the weight of it drags me right over onto the floor. I fall hard on my elbow. Pain shoots through my arm, and all I want to do is curl up and hide in the supply closet for the rest of the day. But that's not a thing you can attempt around here more than once. In fact, as I found out last week, you can get in a lot of trouble if you do.

First period is history, and Ms. Cross is already standing at the blackboard. She's got our textbook, *The American Vision, Volume One: New England,* propped open in one hand and yellow chalk dust all over her pants. As usual, her pants are tucked into waterproof boots, like she's ready to go duck hunting at a moment's notice, and everybody's scrambling to keep up with the notes. She doesn't even say anything about me being late; she just takes off her owl glasses and gives me her disappointed look. Then she pops the glasses back on her face and picks up her chalk. "All right! Where were we, scholars?"

The thing about Ms. Cross is that her ancestors

were witnesses for the prosecution during a famous witch trial in Maine and she's never really gotten over it. She teaches history now with this sort of supernatural determination, as if it were her destiny, as if every time she tells the story to another group of kids, she's getting closer somehow to setting things right and erasing the stain on her family's history.

Emma Bishop, my mortal enemy, already has her hand up, and she's waving it around, desperate to be called on.

"Yes, Miss Bishop?"

"We were discussing Judge Bishop's ruling in the trial of Hannah Martin."

Unlike Ms. Cross, Emma harbors no remorse whatsoever about her own family's ruthlessness during the witch trials. In fact, ruthlessness is a trait that she, newly appointed captain of our middle school's gymnastics team, seems to share with her infamous ancestor.

"Yes. Now, look." Ms. Cross taps her chalk against a map of Maine. "The thing to remember when we talk about witches is always this issue of *who* gets labeled a witch and *why*. You see, sometimes labels tell us less about the person being labeled and more about the culture that assigns them a label in the first place."

Last week, in preparation for the Salt and Stars Folk Festival, we skipped ahead in *The American Vision*, all the way to chapter 35, to a section called "Multiculturalism: Folklore and Rituals Around the World." Ms. Cross told us to pay special attention to the similarities between the rituals we found there because they prove that "some questions are universal and essential to the human experience." My favorite was the Japanese Obon festival, when family members light lanterns and float them on the water to guide the spirits of the dead and help them find their way home. Ms. Cross even had us make our own paper lanterns and place them around the classroom so we could see what they looked like.

I heard some parents complained about that unit, but I thought it was the best we'd ever done.

The worst was chapter 1, "New Beginnings," which was about colonists coming over from England seeking religious freedom and a better life. I swear, we couldn't get through one single paragraph without Emma announcing which prominent colonial figures she was related to.

"I have a very historical family," she told us.

"I mean, who doesn't?" I muttered.

But I knew what she meant. She meant she has the kind of family that gets written about in a text-book.

I kept thinking we'd eventually get to something on my own ancestors, but the further we read in chapter one, the bleaker it looked. In the end, all we got was one small sidebar titled "Native Americans," which might as well have been titled "Magical Tree Sprites" for all the useful information it provided. I mean, I've never met my mother's family, but I do know that they are members of the Penobscot Nation and that they currently live on a reservation outside Old Town, not too far from Starbridge Cove. Also, I'm pretty sure their ancestors didn't just magically appear in the forest when the colonists arrived. Like, I'm sure they had their own things going on, just like the colonists did. Things they worried about, and things they loved, and things they were build-ing, and things that scared them. We just never read about that in school.

Right now we're up to chapter 3: "Witchcraft Comes to New England."

"Now, let's return to the deposition of Samuel Peach. You will find his original testimony, in Colonial English, reprinted in your textbook on page eighty-two. For now, to expedite our discussion, I will read you an abridged version." Ms. Cross pushes her glasses farther up the bridge of her nose and begins to read: "'Sworn May the eleventh: 1692: The deponent saw Hannah Martin come in at the window. She was in her hood and scarf and the same dress that she was in before at meeting the same day. Being come in she drew up his body and lay upon him about an hour and half in all which time this deponent could not stir nor speak, but feeling himself beginning to be loosened or lightened he put out his hand among the clothes and took hold of her hand and brought it up to his mouth and bit three of the fingers (as he judge) to the breaking of the bones.'"*

---

* Deposition of Bernard Peach: http://salem.lib.virginia.edu/texts/tei/swp?term= Bernard%20Peach&div_id=n92.12&chapter_id=n92. (Essex County Archives, Salem— Witchcraft Vol. I Page 65)

"Now." She looks up. "Who believes this testimony? Anyone?"

"Judge Bishop did."

"That's right." She takes a step closer and her glasses slide a little down her nose.

"But what about you, Miss Salt? Do you believe Samuel Peach found Hannah Martin in his bedroom that night and broke three of her fingers, bit right through them, because she cast a spell on him that he was trying to escape?"

"No." I pull my braid back over my shoulder and start twining my hair around my finger. "That doesn't make any sense."

"Well, I should think not. And what made her so vulnerable, to him and to the town's hysteria?"

"She . . . well, she lived by herself, and she didn't have any family in the village. Also, she wasn't born there or in England. She was from Barbados."

"And what about the trial? What exactly did Judge Bishop have to say about the whole thing?"

I glance up. "I don't know."

"Well, did you finish reading the chapter? On what are you basing your information, Miss Salt?"

Emma turns around in her seat. "Maybe she's a witch."

Ms. Cross keeps her eyes on me. "Miss Salt, take out your book. And for goodness' sake, take out something to write with! How do you people ever expect to learn anything if you don't have the proper materials? This is *middle school*."

I take another deep breath and open my bag. As a siren-in-training, I'm always losing things and running late, so I use the same bag for everything. Inside, I have the usual school stuff: binders, folders, a collection of pink pens, crumpled papers, tissues, a travel mug, vanilla hand cream, cherry ChapStick, watermelon gum, hair bands, and gym shoes. But then I also have my siren stuff, things we've scavenged from shipwrecks for the Sea Witch: buttons, and sea glass, and antique jewelry. Plus a few stolen library books to read if I get bored during algebra. When I finally locate my copy of *The American Vision*, the entire thing is coffee stained and ripped apart.

Ms. Cross has completely abandoned the board and is now standing directly in front of me, staring in horror. "Miss Salt," she says, "that bag is

bigger than you are. How do you ever find anything?"

"Yeah," Emma agrees. "And her *American Vision*
is a total disaster."

"That's quite enough, Miss Bishop," Ms. Cross
shushes her. "You keep your eyes on your own
American Vision. Now, Miss Salt, I'm going to need
to see you after school." She pops the glasses back
on. "And for goodness' sake, don't be late!"

"Okay." I pull the rubber band from my braid
and let my hair fall in front of my face.

The bell sounds then, and class is over. That bell
is another thing I hate about middle school. First of
all, it's extremely alarming. You'd think there was a
major bank robbery in progress every time it goes
off, which is exactly eight times per day. Also, when
it rings, everybody stops what they're doing and
starts shoving books and binders back in their bags,
no matter what's going on. Even if the teacher is
telling you something important.

"Students!" Ms. Cross holds up her hands.
"Wait until I dismiss you, please." But it's useless.
That bell is more powerful than any teacher, and
the teachers sort of know it.

† † †

We all pour out into the hallway and stream along to our next class. For me, second period is gym, and I dread it. It's not the physical activity that I mind; it's the ten minutes we have to spend changing into sneakers and shorts. The thing about our type of sirens is that in addition to our silvery hair, we all have these gross green scales on the bottom of our feet. As we get older, our scales get brighter and thicker, and then they extend out in a spiral pattern and wrap all the way up our ankles. According to my research, the scales are supposed to make it easier for us to climb and navigate the slippery rocks of the northern New England coastline. They do not, however, make it easier to navigate a middle school locker room.

I think my scales are basically the most embarrassing thing in the world, and I spend a significant amount of time planning my outfits to conceal them. Of course, my sisters wear their scales proudly. They tell everyone they're some kind of artsy tattoo, and everybody believes it and admires them. Up at the high school, girls are painting snakeskin patterns on their ankles and gluing green glitter on top of their feet. But I'm not nearly brave enough to try that myself. I stick to kneesocks.

The locker room is all concrete cinder blocks and steel lockers, with wire mesh over the windows and clocks. It's sort of like a jail cell, except the air is thick with the scent of artificial fruit from everybody's body lotion. I always change in the corner with all the girls who have stuff to hide, like if they're not wearing a bra yet or they don't use deodorant or shave their legs.

Today, instead of a real gym class, we're having a dress rehearsal for the festival. The whole school is going to be marching in the parade and participating in an interpretive dance choreographed by our own Coach Bouchard. Each grade has a different theme, and although he probably wouldn't admit it, I'm fairly certain that Coach Bouchard assigned us all parts based on our personalities and physical characteristics. The seventh-grade theme is "Sea Mammals and Shellfish." I am playing the role of a snail.

Of course, Emma changes right up front, by

the mirror. She gets to be a mermaid in the festival, which doesn't even make any sense. Coach Bouchard overheard me telling Jason about it the other day. The eighth-grade theme is "Indigenous Foliage," and Jason was dressed up as a pinecone. "You know," I told him, "mermaids aren't even shellfish."

Coach Bouchard shook his head. "They're mammals, I guess."

I looked up at him. "They are?"

"Of course."

"How do you know?"

He chuckled and flipped his hair back. He's tall and has really long hair that he usually keeps tied back in a ponytail. He also rides a motorcycle around town on Sunday afternoons, and he's been known to say things like "groovy" in response to the girls' lacrosse team winning the state championship. I think the ponytail and the motorcycle are a little silly, but the thing I like about Coach Bouchard is that he never gets too mad when I complain about stuff or have a bad attitude— which, I have to admit, is pretty much always. "Lolly, part of participating in the festival is learning to be a team player. Now, you go out there and do the best you can with the part you've been given. Play the hand—or, in this case, the shell—you've been dealt."

As a mermaid, Emma gets to wear a sparkly clamshell bikini top and a long, gauzy skirt, and she's even started bringing her own cheerleader pom-poms from home, because, she explains, she likes to "go the extra mile." I, on the other hand, have to wear antennae and a cardboard shell strapped to my back. Anyway, I'm pretty certain that nobody ever heard of a mermaid cheerleader.

Today, Emma changes into her costume and then hops up on the bench to tack a flyer to the highest point of the bulletin board.

IMPORTANT ANNOUNCEMENTS!
SAILING TRYOUTS: TODAY!
HOMECOMING DANCE: FRIDAY NIGHT!
HALLOWEEN REGATTA: OCTOBER 31ST!

Then, instead of just climbing down from the bench, she decides to perform a cartwheel that ends with her in a full split on the concrete floor. Everyone gathers around and applauds.

"I can do that," I whisper.

Emma gets up and puts her hands on her hips. "What did you say?"

I finish rolling up my kneesocks and straighten my antennae. "I said I can do that."

"Yeah, right. You're just a snail. Anyone who can do that would be on the gymnastics team and playing a mermaid in the festival."

"First of all, mermaids can't even do gymnastics. They don't have legs. And secondly, I *was* on the gymnastics team. I had to quit."

"Why?"

"Because I—I had other things to do." I turn away from her and start struggling into my shell.

"Oh." She sniffs. *"Things."*

"I have to help at my family's diner."

"That's cool." You can tell by her tone that she doesn't think it's remotely cool.

"Just watch."

She stands back. "Go ahead."

I put my shell down on the floor and sink into a split to match hers.

"Whatever," she says. "Any snail could do that. That just means you're flexible. That's not gymnastics."

I stand up and brush my hands off on my shorts. "What do you want me to do, then?"

"I dare you to do a back walkover. Here. Down the aisle."

"Fine." I look at the floor for a second, calculating, and then I turn around and arch my back until my hands are planted on the floor. It's a move I've done a million times before and on much trickier surfaces than this. But then, right as I kick my legs up and start to flip over, my injured elbow sends a wave of electricity up my arm, and the next thing I know, I'm lying on the ground with my cardboard shell crumpled beneath me.

Everyone is watching.

Emma is standing there shaking her ponytail. "That was a total disaster," she says, like I don't already know it. "I really think you should just stick to being a snail."

"What's going on in here?" Couch Bouchard is suddenly on the scene, shoving his way through the crowd, blowing his whistle in sharp, short blasts. "You girls were all supposed to be out there five minutes ago! Lolly, why are you on the floor?"

"She tried to do a back walkover," Emma explains. "But she didn't make it."

"Thanks, Emma." Couch Bouchard pats her on the shoulder. "That's useful information." Then he bends over and blows his whistle in my ear. "Lolly! Did you hit your head?"

I sit up slowly. "No. I fell on my shell."

He blows his whistle again to signal that he's finished dealing with our nonsense, and then he waves everybody out of the locker room. "Okay, let's go, ladies! Emma, you take Lolly to see Nurse Claire." He reaches into the pocket of his wind pants and pulls out a blank pad of paper and a miniature pencil. "I'll write her a note so she knows what happened."

"Is she coming back?" Emma asks.

"What do you mean?"

"Lolly. I mean, she looks pretty hurt. She should probably take her bag and stuff in case she needs to stay with the nurse all period. Or

even, like, go home or something for the day.
I'll carry it for her."

"Sure, Emma. Thank you. That's good thinking."

We make it about three quarters of the way to the
nurse's office before we get in a fight. I'm still
wearing my snail antennae and Emma's still wearing her sparkly mermaid bikini. She's carrying my
bag like she can't wait to toss it out the front door.
"You might have been a big deal in elementary
school," she explains. "You know, because of gymnastics and your sisters. But it's not the same
here."

"I don't think I'm a big deal."

She glances at me. "I know what you said
about me."

"What are you talking about? What did I say?"

"Don't try to deny it. Jason told me everything.
He and I are really good friends now, in case you
didn't notice."

We reach Nurse Claire's office and stop walking.

"But I didn't say anything!"

"I think you're lying."

Lula always tells me that if I'm ever in an

argument with a really mean girl, I should just look her in the eye and say, simply: *Ew.* I've never tried it before, but this seems like the right time.

I narrow my eyes and put my hands on my hips. "Ew."

It works. Emma is momentarily speechless, and you can tell she's racking her brain for what to say next. But then she thinks of something. "You know the whole town thinks your mom drove off that bridge on purpose."

"What are you talking about? That's not true."

"It said in the police report that she was speeding. She was going, like, fifty miles an hour when she plowed into the barrier. My parents read about it in the paper. I mean, my cousin works at Sunrise County General, and everybody knows your mom was checked in there half the time you said she was on tour, so it all kind of made sense. And now your dad won't even live in the same house as you."

"He does too live in our house! He has an apartment upstairs from the diner because he needs to practice his music."

"Yeah, sure. Everybody knows that your dad

doesn't want anything to do with you guys. He's, like, too cool for you."

"He's not too cool for us!"

"Whatever, *snail*!"

"I'm not a snail!"

"Girls!" Nurse Claire opens the door and glares at us like we're a couple of sea monsters that just crawled out of the cafeteria sink. That's the worst thing about turning twelve. Suddenly adults stop looking at you like you're a harmless little kid and start looking at you like you're a potentially explosive device and they're not sure whether to disarm you or duck under a table. "There are students in here trying to take naps! Now, what is all this commotion? You can't just walk down the hallway yelling like this."

Emma hands her the note. "This is from Coach Bouchard," she says. "Lolly fell on her arm."

Nurse Claire leans against the doorjamb while she reads the note. She's recently started wearing high heels and dangly silver earrings with her lab coat, which I think looks really weird. "Wait here, please," she tells us and shuts the door.

Emma and I sit next to each other on the bench

between the nurse's office and the principal's office with our bodies aimed as far from each other as the bench will allow. She has her arms folded across her chest and her legs crossed, and I have my feet up and my arms wrapped around my knees. We hold on to ourselves and look off in separate directions.

I try to concentrate on how much I dislike Emma instead of on the throbbing pain in my elbow. Her parents own Bishop's Fish, a big company that exports lobsters and "other fine seafood" to places like Las Vegas and Cleveland. We've always competed against each other in gymnastics, but we officially became mortal enemies on the first day of coed volleyball. Jason was captain, and he chose us both to be on his team. But he chose me first. And then Emma proceeded to serve a volleyball into the back of my head. Coach Bouchard ruled it an accident, but the whole class saw, and we all knew what it meant. First of all, Emma Bishop is the most athletic person in our grade. There's pretty much zero chance of her not being able to serve a volleyball over a net. And secondly, she might make it look that way, but

Emma never does anything by accident. It was, as Ms. Cross would say, "a shot over the bow."

Finally, Nurse Claire returns. "Emma," she says. "Your mother will pick you up after sailing practice today, and she'll be stopping by for a conversation with me about all these little fights you've been getting into."

"What little fights?"

"We'll talk after school. Lolly, nobody is home at your house. Please have your father call me at his earliest convenience."

Emma raises her hand, very professional, like we're still in class. "May I return to gym now?"

Nurse Claire nods and avoids making eye contact with her. Sometimes, even adults are scared of Emma. "Yes you may."

Emma walks away without giving either of us a second look.

Nurse Claire waves me into the office. "Come on, Lolly," she says. "Let's fix up that arm."

I follow her into the office and climb up on one of the plastic cots. My legs dangle over the side, and my antennae bob up and down.

Nurse Claire starts pulling supplies out of the

cabinet. A flashlight. A sling. A thermometer. She works part-time at my old elementary school, so we've known each other forever. When I was little, I used to love going to her office. Whatever was bothering me, a fever or a scraped knee, she'd make it better. And then she'd let me take a candy from the ceramic dish on her desk. Sometimes I'd even pretend to be sick just so I could go and see her. Of course, things are different now. Nurse Claire doesn't even keep candy on her desk at this school. It's all business here.

Nurse Claire takes my arm in her hands and extends it gently, feeling the bones with her fingers. I close my eyes for a second and pretend she's my mom. I can't help it.

"Gosh, you're cold," she says. "Your skin is like ice. Are you feeling sick?"

"No." I shake my head. "It's always like that."

"Lolly, I'm actually glad you're here. I've been meaning to speak to you about something. Several of your teachers have mentioned your recent"—she lowers her voice—"*behavior problems.* There's talk of attention issues, sleepiness, organizational difficulties. Skipping class. Now, you've always been such a good student. What's going on?"

"Oh." I'd like to tell her that there is a very simple explanation for all of those behaviors and it's a little thing called "becoming a siren." *Excuse me,* I'd like to say, *but I'm becoming a siren. I'm becoming a siren, and I want desperately to stop. Can you help me with that?* But I obviously can't say that. And anyway, this isn't a problem that she can fix with tongue depressors and candy. Things aren't that simple anymore. "I guess I haven't been sleeping that well lately."

She lets go of my arm.

"How are your sisters?"

"Fine."

"Lily's doing okay? Settling in at the high school?"

"I think so."

"Well, here. Before I forget—" She goes to the wall and retrieves a pamphlet with a picture of a dead tree on the cover. It's called *Grief: The Significance of the First Year.* "I've been meaning to share this with you. I think you and your sisters might find it helpful."

"Thanks." I slide the pamphlet into my bag.

"Will you be going to the dance on Friday?"

"What does that have to do with anything?"

"Oh." She laughs, and her earrings dangle. "I was just checking. I'll be a chaperone this year."

"I think I have to work. I mean, I have to help out at the diner. Friday nights are busy for us."

"I see. Well, this is just a bruise."

"Can I keep it in a sling?" I point to the half-open cabinet where she keeps ACE bandages and tape. "I think I'd feel safer that way."

She nods. "If you want to. Don't be afraid to move it around, though, you know? You don't want it freezing up on you."

"I know," I tell her.

"Lolly." She pauses for a moment with the sling in her hands. "Remember in fourth grade when your mom had to go away for a while? You insisted that your leg was in excruciating pain and kept coming to my office wanting to borrow a set of crutches."

"Yes," I tell her. "I remember."

"But really," she continues, "there was nothing wrong. Your leg was perfectly fine."

"This isn't like that," I assure her. "But if you don't want me to use the sling, I won't. It's fine. I just want to go back to class now." Before I fall off this table and die of embarrassment.

"No, here." She hands me the sling. "You're welcome to it. It's just . . . there's nothing wrong with looking for support and attention, you know, in other ways. It doesn't always have to be a physical problem. We could talk about other things that are bothering you too."

"Okay, well, thank you." I slip into the sling and grab my bag with my other hand. "This will be good enough for now."

I'm never coming back here again.

"And, Lolly? Try not to let Emma get to you, okay? You girls—it's like you hit twelve years old and you all become little monsters."

At the end of the day, I walk to Ms. Cross's classroom and lean in the doorway. She's just sitting at her desk grading papers, but I can't figure out what to say to let her know I'm there. *Hi? Excuse me?* Nothing seems right. It's like the connection between my brain and my mouth has been cut, and all I want to do is turn and run away. It's funny how I was never this nervous around my teachers in elementary school. There, I was always just myself. And I knew exactly who that was, too. Lorelei Elizabeth Salt: vocabulary quiz champion, proud member of the highest reading group, rising star of the JV gymnastics team. But here I have all these secrets to keep. I have to pretend to be somebody I'm not, and honestly, it's exhausting.

Thankfully, Ms. Cross looks up then and sees me standing there. "Miss Salt." She glances at the clock. "You're right on time! Please, come in."

"I can't." I nod at my elbow. "I just came to tell you that I have to cancel my detention. I'm injured."

"I see." She glances back down at her desk and shuffles some papers. "You realize, of course, that students are not allowed to cancel their own detentions."

"Yes," I tell her, even though I actually didn't know that.

"Well," she continues, "I've been here for a long time. I have a little leeway with the administration. How does tomorrow sound?"

"I don't know." I look up at my Obon lantern, hanging slightly apart from the others by the far corner. I had to climb a bookshelf to get it up there, but I wanted it as high and as close to the window as possible. "I'll have to see how I feel."

She looks at me for a moment with this wondering expression, like she recognizes me from some other place and she's waiting for me to explain how exactly it is that we know each other. "All right, then." She picks up a pen and starts circling things. "Come back when you're ready."

"I will," I promise. And I mean it. There's something about how calm and unhurried she is that actually kind of makes me want to stay, that makes me think maybe this is a place where I could sit for ten seconds without a bell ringing, or a locker slamming, or a volleyball flying at my head.

"Have a good evening, dear. Feel better."

"Thanks, Ms. Cross. You too."

On my way back down the hall, I stop by the water fountain. Outside, the sun is starting to set, and the hallway is filled with dusty, tangerine-colored light. It's already starting to get dark early. Soon the cold and the blizzards will set in, and then people won't even want to leave their houses. I think that's why the Salt and Stars Folk Festival is so important around here. It's like our last gasp of summer.

There's a boy standing by the lockers. He looks familiar, but his profile is in shadow. I move a few steps closer and realize that it's Jason. "Hey!" I call to him and wave. "I almost didn't recognize you. You're still here?"

"Yup. Sailing tryouts start in fifteen minutes."

And then Emma comes around the corner. She's traded her cheerleader-mermaid attire for a red polo shirt, shorts, and a matching visor. Emma has the right outfit for everything. She's a lot like Jason that way. "Ready?"

I feel like I'm living some sort of nightmare. "Ready for what?"

"I'm not talking to you, Lolly." She loops her arm through Jason's. "We're going sailing."

"Wait, you're going sailing—together?"

Jason clears his throat. "She's on my team."

"You have a team?"

"Yes, we have a team. And we're going to win the regatta too."

"You know . . . Jason doesn't even like sailing." I can feel myself losing my temper. It happens to me all the time lately, like the world starts speeding up and all I can feel is how mad I am, and then I blurt out the first thing that comes into my head. "He gets seasick!"

Jason's eyes grow huge and his face turns pink. "Lolly, stop!"

"Well, I just thought she should know."

Jason pulls his arm away from Emma and retreats to the safety of the boys' bathroom.

Emma rolls her eyes. "Nice work," she says. "You know, we're not little kids anymore. Just because you and Jay were best friends in elementary school doesn't mean you are here."

"Whatever." I say it as if it doesn't bother me at all, as if I couldn't care less about their budding friendship and their winning team. I sound pretty convincing, too. I mean, if I overheard myself, I'd probably be intimidated. Maybe. But still, as I turn and walk away down the hall, my stomach hurts.

She called him Jay. I can't stop thinking about the new nickname. *When did that start? Do other people call him that? How did I not know about this?* I pause in front of a shoe store on Main Street and pretend to become absorbed in a display of high-heeled shoes. Instead, I stare at my reflection in the display window, at the silvery streaks growing brighter and brighter and the dark hollows under my eyes. A woman in a long flowered dress strolls past, strumming a painted guitar, and I watch her reflection too. Another singer rehearsing for the festival. She's playing an old French folk song, one of our mom's favorites, which just makes me feel even worse. Mom used to say that's the problem with living in a town full of folksingers: somebody's always singing the blues.

Five o'clock rolls around and there's no sign of Jason. I wait by the kitchen door for a few minutes, standing on tiptoe, searching for the flash of his blue raincoat against the orange maple leaves. But he's nowhere to be seen.

Lara comes up behind me and pats my shoulder. "How's the arm?"

"It hurts a little."

"How long do you have to wear the sling?"

"Nurse Claire said probably till tomorrow. You know, just to be safe."

Lara nods. "No visitor today?"

I shake my head. "No. Guess not."

"Think you can still carry a few sodas for me?"

"Sure."

"Take these up to the register, then." She slips three dripping cans of soda into my hands. "Ms. Cross is here for her order."

Ms. Cross comes to the diner almost every evening on her way home from work, and every night she orders two Diet Cokes and two turkey sandwiches on whole wheat bread, and she always leaves a tip even though she takes them to go. I haven't figured out yet who the other sandwich is for.

I balance the cans against each other, which is a trick my sisters taught me for carrying multiple beverages without a tray, and hurry out of the kitchen. A few tables from the front, I skid to a stop. Jason's stepfather, Mr. Bergstrom, is sitting at the counter on the other side of the frosted glass divider, talking to Emma's dad and holding an upside-down ketchup bottle over an order of fries. The two of them are bulky in knit caps, jackets, and layers of flannel shirts, perched like seagulls on their stools.

I wouldn't call us mortal enemies exactly, but Jason's stepfather and I don't get along. Not since the afternoon he discovered a secret stockpile of junk food I'd created in Jason's bedroom. Mr. Bergstrom has this thing against store-bought snacks and he doesn't allow them in his house. And when he married Jason's mom, he decided that Jason wasn't going to be allowed to have store-bought snacks anymore either. As he explained, "You're not living in a trailer anymore, and you're not going to eat like you are. Your mother will be providing us with home-cooked meals now instead of all that junk."

Jason probably would have gone along with the snack embargo, the way he goes along with most things. Only, I decided it wasn't fair. I mean, Jason is a very picky eater, and store-bought snacks are some of the few foods he likes. So I started getting Lara to buy them for us: sleeves of cookies, and brightly colored bags of chips, and treats in shiny blue foil. And soon, Jason had an entire drawer filled with secret emergency snacks.

Everything was working out fine until one afternoon when Mr. Bergstrom opened the door to Jason's room and caught us opening the secret snack drawer.

We thought maybe he would yell at us or throw things. We'd seen what he was like when he was angry at his own kids. But he didn't. Instead, he just went and got a garbage bag, and then he scooped up all of our snacks and sent me home with them like a disgraced Santa Claus. And then he called Lara and told her that he hoped I'd learned my lesson because if I broke any more of his rules, I'd be banned from their home faster than a sleeve of cookies.

"This is nothing to do with the safety of the port, Tom," he's saying now, whacking the ketchup bottle with his palm. "Starbridge Cove is still a fine place to dock a ship and has been since the seventeenth century. There's history here."

"Of course, Erik. Nobody's denying that. And nobody wants to see this town succeed more than I do. But I have a business to run as well, and I cannot afford another wreck like this morning. You know how it is. The repairs cost a fortune. I'll just take my business down to Portland if I have to."

"Listen to me." Mr. Bergstrom puts the ketchup bottle down. "There was a problem this morning. I'll admit that. There is a problem out there right now. But I know what it is, and I will take care of it. Trust me."

"Well, I'd like to. I sure would." Mr. Bishop clears his throat and sprinkles salt on his own fries. "Money is at issue here, though, and I—"

Mr. Bergstrom looks as if he'd like to upend the fries all over Mr. Bishop's lap. "Tom, I don't want to see any more harm come to your fleet. That's your livelihood, just the way the harbor at Starbridge Cove is mine. But how can you be so sure that if you take that step, if you take your business down to Portland, your fleet will still be safe? The coastline in this state is nothing if not rocky. Unpredictable. There's no telling what could happen at any time."

Mr. Bishop brings a fry to his mouth as if he means to take a bite, then thinks better of it and puts it back in the basket. "Are you threatening me?"

"My family's owned this port for generations.

Now, I've acknowledged there's a bit of a problem out there right now, and I intend to take care of it. Let me do my job."

"You think it's sirens, don't you? You believe the old stories."

"Don't you?" Mr. Bergstrom leans forward, and the glare from the neon sign through the window casts an ugly green glow on his face. His left eye is swollen and bruised. "You know it as well as I do. There have always been certain . . . forces in our midst."

"Even if that were true, you think you can find them? And stop them?"

"I know I can."

"How?"

"There is a certain type of young lady we're looking for, a group of them, a group of girls with special musical abilities."

"My daughter just performed a solo in the choir last Sunday." Mr. Bishop starts eating again and speaks with his mouth full of fries. "That doesn't make her a siren."

"The sirens of Starbridge Cove are not singing in any church choir, I assure you." Mr. Bergstrom lowers his voice and leans closer to Mr. Bishop. "Look, you know what I mean when I say that we are a certain type of community here. A close-knit community. When we talk about sirens, we're not talking about girls like your daughter. These are outsiders, girls who lurk in the shadows. They're sneaking around out there, watching us. They're casting spells and composing songs. Little anarchists, plotting our demise. These are girls with the power to read your mind and craft a song, a lie, that speaks to the deepest, most secret wishes of your heart. Now, as I said, my family's been dealing with these monsters for decades. From time to time, a group of them crops up and tries to cause trouble. It's never lasted, though. We know how to handle them."

Before I can stop it, one of the cans of soda slips from my fingers and explodes against the floor. It makes a sound like a gunshot. By the front door, Ms. Cross actually screams and covers her head with her hands.

"Lolly!" Lily rushes over with a roll of paper towels. She kneels and starts blotting the spill. "What is wrong with you?"

"Nothing!"

Mr. Bergstrom and Mr. Bishop both stand up partway and peer at us over the divider.

"I was just bringing these to the front," I explain.

"Well, stop standing there staring into space."

Lara comes over and swats at Lily with her apron. "Go get more soda, Lily."

"But she—"

"Just go! Lolly, what's wrong now?"

"I need to talk to you." I grab Lara's hand and pull her into the bathroom.

In the bathroom, under the fluorescent lights, Lara looks a lot older than eighteen. "We're right in the middle of the dinner rush, Lolly. Lula's gonna kill me if I leave her out there alone."

"But there's something really bad happening."

She checks her watch. "You have seven seconds."

"Mr. Bergstrom is here, and I just heard him saying that he knows all about sirens. He says he's hunted them before and he knows that they're back. He's getting ready to hunt them again."

Lara folds her arms across her chest and leans

against the wall. She shuts her eyes for a second, and I bet she feels like she could just fall asleep right there against the cool green tiles. I know I could. Then she opens her eyes again and puts her hand on my head. "It'll be okay," she says. "The Sea Witch is stronger than he is. We are stronger than he is. He's always acting like a fool. You know that. He's all talk."

"I don't like him, Lara. He's really mean to Jason and—"

"That's not our business, Lolly. Now stop worrying, okay? Like I just said, he's all talk. Look, your shift is almost over. Why don't you go home and do some homework?"

"I don't want to be home alone. Can I go to Jason's?"

"Okay, sure. But stay out of trouble, all right? And stop antagonizing his dad. I don't want any more angry phone calls from him about you."

"Stepdad," I remind her.

"Right," she says. "Look, Mr. Bergstrom's a jerk, but just because something's unfair doesn't mean you have to be the one to fix it. It's okay to let go of things some of the time, Lolly. Stop trying to right all the wrongs, and just do your algebra homework."

Back in the kitchen, I untie my apron and slip my arm out of the sling. I toss them both over the coatrack and slide a bag of potato chips into the pocket of my rain jacket because, despite what Mr. Bergstrom thinks, I have not learned my lesson.

Halfway to Jason's house, when I can no longer see the lights from the town, I wander down toward the water. It's getting dark out, and the wind off the water is cold. I pull my fingers into my sleeves and let the waves creep up to the toes of my boots. A little farther on, I stop to investigate a washed-up fish skeleton and pick up a seashell shaped like a star. I think my mom would have liked to see it. She and I had a whole seashell collection, and we did all these art projects with them, like taking a hot glue gun and sticking them onto mugs and plates. That's the reason none of our kitchen stuff matches. It drives Lily crazy, but Mom and I liked it that way.

Overhead, seagulls float, calling to each other and dive-bombing the ocean. The outdoor stage is already set up, and I can hear the Ukrainian folk music troupe, Baba Yaga, rehearsing. I can't understand exactly what the song's about because they sing mostly in Ukrainian, but Dad says all folk music is really the music of the oppressed, music that expresses secret things, like subversive political statements and plans to overthrow the ruling class.

The lead singer of Baba Yaga stands about seven feet tall. He sings with his eyes closed while stomping his feet and playing an accordion, and the music cartwheels and flips from his body. It bends and splits and arabesques through the air. To me, folk music sounds just the way gymnastics feels, and I can't help it: I throw myself forward into a cartwheel, planting my palms in the firm wet sand, and I let the feeling of flying take over. Just for a second, arms and legs outstretched, I completely forget where I am. Who I am. It's like my entire body is mine again and I could come right side up and find that I'm just a normal girl, and my mom is still here, and Jason isn't mad at me, and nothing is lost.

Then my arm starts to hurt, and I let myself fall onto the sand. The lead singer of Baba Yaga is watching, smiling at me. He gives me a wave and an enthusiastic thumbs-up, and I lift my hair out of my eyes and wave back.

I keep walking until the shoreline curves and the beach starts looking a lot cleaner and the houses start getting a lot bigger. This is the part of town where Emma Bishop lives. And now Jason lives here too. At Jason's house, all of the walls are windows, and nearly every window has a view of the sea. The house is surrounded by a walkway made entirely of crushed shells and smooth white pebbles, like a moat.

Once upon a time, Jason's mom was a waitress at the diner, which is how he and I met. But now she doesn't have to work. Now she spends most of her time lying in a lounge chair on the widow's walk that circles the third floor of the house. In summer, she sips cold drinks and reads magazines up there, and she always has her nails painted bright red and wears a bathing suit and sunglasses that match. After Labor Day, she trades her summer accessories for a monogrammed mug of tea and a fashionable plaid shawl, which she alternates wearing as a scarf, a blanket, and a cape, and which is made of the softest material I've ever felt in my life. Tonight, she has it draped over her shoulders, and she gathers it in one hand and waves when she sees me approaching, my footsteps crunching up the walkway. Her long, penny-colored hair comes loose and whips across her face.

I wave back. "Hi, Alice!"

I like Jason's mom. She is like a princess in a fairy tale.

Inside the house, the air-conditioning is still blasting, as usual. No matter how hot it is outside, that house is always freezing cold. And then it takes Jason's stepdad about a month longer than the rest of the town to shut it down for winter. Jason even complained about it once, but Alice explained that because of his hunting trophies, Mr. Bergstrom is very sensitive about humidity. And very insensitive to the needs of everybody else, in my opinion.

I rub the goose bumps on my arms and head down the hall. Jason's three stepbrothers are playing video games in the living room, shouting and pushing each other.

I walk up the massive winding staircase to

Jason's room and lean in the doorway. His room is neat, as always. His bed is made, his books are arranged in alphabetical order, and his walls are covered in nautical maps and posters from old marine biology textbooks, all displayed as precisely as if his bedroom were an art gallery. Jason has always kept his stuff like that, even when he and his mom were living in their tiny trailer and sleeping on a pullout couch.

Jason is sitting on the floor with a book and a strand of rope in his fingers. He's bent forward in concentration, so his hair, the color of rust and grown too long, falls over his eyes. He's needed a haircut for a while, but nobody around there ever seems to notice. His radio is on as usual, playing WCOD, the folk rock station.

"What are you doing?" I ask.

He looks up at me. "Practicing. I need to be able to tie these sailor's knots for the race." He shuts the book and pushes it aside. "What happened to your arm? Why did you have it in a sling before?"

"Oh," I tell him. "I fell. But it's okay now."

He nods and looks back down at his rope.

"So you made it, then? You qualified?"

"Yeah. We made it."

I pull the door shut and slide his desk chair in front of it, just in case. Then I take a seat next to him on the floor and drop the bag of chips into his lap. "Sorry I was sort of mean before."

He smiles and pushes the chips under his bed. "That's okay."

"I just don't understand why you're changing."

"I'm not changing." He runs his hands through his hair and it falls right back in his face. "I'm getting better."

"Yeah, but you get seasick. You can't help that."

He shrugs. "I don't know. Maybe I don't really get seasick. Maybe that's not the real reason I don't like being on the water."

"Then what's the real reason?" I glance at him, but he's already looking the other way. I remember when we were little, Jason always had this extreme quietness about him, especially at school. He'd barely ever talk, and he'd sort of follow me around everywhere. He always seemed pretty content, though, just as long as he knew that his shoes were lined up, and his shirts were hanging the right way, and I was someplace nearby. I was like his protector.

"I don't want to talk about this anymore. It's just time to stop acting like a little kid. I'm almost fourteen years old. I should be able to sail as well as anybody else. I shouldn't be scared anymore. Right?"

No! I feel like stamping my feet and shouting. *I want you to stay right here where it's safe. On dry land.*

But of course, I can't say any of that. So I just pick up a ballpoint pen from the floor and start drawing snail shells on the soles of my boots. "Fine."

Jason changes the subject. "Did you hear there was another accident at the marina last night? Actually, it was early this morning."

I put down the pen. "No, I don't think so. What happened?"

"My stepdad went down to help out and I guess he got hit in the head or something. Half his face is all banged up."

"Oh, really? Well, how . . . how is he doing?"

"He was in the hospital this morning, but he's okay."

"Did they say what happened? I mean, what caused the accident?"

"The storm, I guess. The boat's completely destroyed."

"And he didn't say anything about . . . well, about anything?"

"What are you talking about? What was he supposed to say?"

I shake my head. "Nothing. I'm sorry. I'm glad he's all right."

Jason shrugs. "Me too, I guess."

A song on the radio ends, and the DJ comes back on. *"Folks, this is DJ Burroughs and you're listening to WCOD, the Cod. That was Bob Dylan off his 1965 classic* Highway 61 Revisited, *and now we're going to play some new music for you. This is Oren Salt and the Walking Shades playing their new single, 'On the Ghost Road.' "*

"I like your dad's new song."

"Thanks."

"Are you going to the dance?"

"Probably not."

"You should." Jason walks over to the closet and starts sorting his dress shirts by color. "I mean, it would be good for you to make some friends."

"I guess." I point to an old orange T-shirt that's hanging in the back of the closet. "You still have that?"

"What?"

"Your Little League shirt?"

"Yup." He smiles and takes it off the hanger. "The Starbridge Starfish. You want it? It's too small on me now."

"Okay."

He tosses me the shirt, and I hold it close to my face.

"Are you sure?" I say. "I mean, you don't want to keep it?"

"I'm sure. I was, like, the worst one on the team. Don't you remember? I used to chase butterflies in the outfield."

"You were cute."

He rolls his eyes. "Great. Well, that's not the look I'm going for anymore."

Downstairs, a door opens and slams.

"Jason!" Alice calls from the kitchen. "Dinner in five minutes!"

"You can stay," he tells me. "I mean, if you want to."

"Yeah," I tell him. "I'll stay."

Dinner at Jason's house has become an interesting event. What used to consist of him and his mom, and microwave dinners on collapsible TV trays, has become a formal affair complete with moose antler chandeliers, giant hunks of meat piled high on silver platters, and settings with lace place mats and three forks. Jason's mom calls it "Viking chic," which I think makes about as much sense as Emma's mermaid gymnast.

Back when he and Alice first started dating, Mr. Bergstrom once had my entire family over for dinner, and he took us on a tour of the house, stopping to point out all the animals he'd personally killed and then hung up on the wall like paintings. "That deer weighed well over two hundred pounds when I got him," he told us. "A real monster. I hunted him for days."

"Hunted?" Mom had laughed at him. "But this isn't hunting. Any fool can shoot a deer."

Now everyone has assigned seats: Mr. Bergstrom

goes at the head of the table with Jason's mom right next to him, and Jason and I go next to her. Jason's stepbrothers sit across from us. The chairs are like thrones, taller than I am, and somehow it always takes me twice as long as everyone else to pull mine out and sit down.

Tonight, Mr. Bergstrom watches me the whole time, shaking his head. "You again?"

Aside from his bruised face, he seems very much like his normal self.

Alice starts serving everyone while the stepbrothers try to catch food in their mouths and poke each other with salad forks. I know they all have names, but I can never remember which name goes with which brother.

"Don't you have your own family to eat dinner with, young lady?"

"I invited her," Jason says.

"Is that a thing we do in this family, Jason? Invite people to dinner in my house without checking with me first?"

Alice holds up one hand like she's trying to stop oncoming traffic. "There's plenty of food! Who wants soup?"

She grabs a ladle, and Mr. Bergstrom pats her as she leans over to serve him.

"Is this a gorgeous woman or what?"

Alice clears her throat. "How are you feeling, honey? Your eye looks pretty banged up."

"Oh, much better. Good as new."

"Well, take it easy for a few days, like the doctors said."

"We'll see." He winks and gives her another pat.

Alice smiles. "Why don't you carve the bird?"

"Good idea." Mr. Bergstrom stands up and plunges a fork and carving knife into the chicken. Then he pauses and clears his throat. "Listen up, everyone! While I have you all here, I have some important news. Someone is going to be the master of ceremonies at this year's Salt and Stars Folk Festival." He waggles his eyebrows and takes a long, dramatic drink from his goblet to draw out the suspense. "And that someone is me!"

"Oh, honey!" Jason's mom starts clapping. "That's fantastic."

"What does that mean?" one of Jason's stepbrothers asks.

"Yeah," another pipes up. "That sounds super embarrassing."

"It means I get a place of honor on the lead float," he explains. "And I make the big welcome speech. And I'll finally have a chance to break out *that* little beauty." He points to a locked display case across the room where he keeps his supposedly authentic Viking heirlooms, including warrior helmets and his prized crown. The crown is made of beaten metal, a sort of old, dirty-looking gold color, and you can see all these big round spaces where, back in the twelfth century, it supposedly was encrusted with jewels. Mr. Bergstrom claims it's been handed down in his family for generations, but Jason has a theory that he actually got it at the Viking theme restaurant in Bangor.

"Dad!" one of the stepbrothers exclaims. "You're not actually gonna wear that out in public, are you?"

"You're darn right I am! I'm going to wear it all the way through the parade and into the auditorium for my speech. And I'll tell you something else: I've got the set guy from the community theater working on building me a knarr."

"A what?"

"A knarr. An authentic dragon ship, just like the one that brought our great ancestor, Erik the Red, to New England in the first place."

"This festival is so lame." Another stepbrother reaches across the table and grabs a roll from the bread basket. "Traffic was stopped for ten minutes on Seawall Avenue today, just so Mr. Hale could carry a giant papier-mâché fish across the street."

"People take their floats very seriously, son." Mr. Bergstrom starts carving and distributing the chicken. "It's a time-honored tradition. Besides, summer only lasts for a short time around here. We need to give it a proper good-bye. Now, when the time comes to do so, I for one intend to be riding a knarr." He stabs some meat with the serving fork and points it at me. "What about you, young lady? What's your role?"

"My role?"

"In the festival. What's your role in the festival?"

I look down at my plate. "I'm a snail."

"A what?"

"A snail."

"Oh." Mr. Bergstrom barely conceals his

disgust as he sits down to his plate. "That sounds unattractive. What is it with these ridiculous costumes this year? My own son's a darn pinecone."

"Stepson," Jason murmurs.

Mr. Bergstrom says, "Ali, babe, can you pass the salt?"

"Sure, hon."

Jason's mom passes the salt.

Jason takes a sip of milk and doesn't make eye contact with anyone.

"It's that Coach Bouchard, isn't it? I don't see what teaching a bunch of kids to play lacrosse has to do with the kind of know-how it takes to pull together a really top-notch festival. He's from Canada, right? Some sort of French Canadian or something?"

The third stepbrother groans. "Why do you care so much?"

"Because this is our heritage, son. We're Bergstroms. We're Vikings! And we're proud of it. In fact, Jason, that's what drew me to your mother in the first place, back when she was waiting on me at the diner."

"What did?"

"Her red hair, of course. I could tell she was of good, hearty Viking stock. Just like us."

"We're not Vikings and neither are you."

"I'm talking about our bloodline, son! There is pure Viking running through these veins. Why, every now and then I still get the urge to . . . pillage."

Jason looks down at his plate, where he's taken care to ensure that none of his separate food groups are touching. "I think I'm gonna throw up."

"That delicate stomach of yours. Well, it's time to toughen up." Mr. Bergstrom pulls the ladle from a bowl of gravy and pours gravy all over Jason's plate. "You know, someday you four boys will inherit my whole company. Viking Industries. The condos, the marina, everything! What do you say?"

Jason shoves the plate away. "I don't want to work for you."

"Then what exactly do you plan to do with your life?"

"I'm going to be a lobsterman, like my real father."

Mr. Bergstrom starts laughing so hard he nearly chokes. "A lobsterman? You can barely set foot on a boat! They'll have no patience for you, Jason." He takes a drink from his goblet. "You think they're going to let you wash your hands fifty times a day out at sea?"

I take a sip of my water. "Our history teacher, Ms. Cross, says it's a source of debate, you know, whether there were ever actually Vikings in the Maine territories. It's not actually been proven."

"And what about you?" Mr. Bergstrom points at me again, this time with the sharp end of his knife. "What's your background? Kind of hard to tell, if you ask me."

Jason sighs. "We didn't ask you."

"Um, my mother was Native American, a member of the Penobscot Nation. My dad's Jewish."

"Oh." Mr. Bergstrom looks even more disgusted than when he found out I was a snail. "No pure bloodlines there."

"No." I resist the urge to apologize for my role at their dinner table.

"Native American, eh?"

"Yes. She was born on the reservation near Old Town."

"And your father's family?"

"They came here a long time ago from Romania."

"Peasants? That sort of thing?"

"I guess so. They used to run a store, like a supermarket, where the diner is now."

"I see. Well, that explains your *look*."

I nod, even though I have no idea what he's talking about. "Yeah."

"Her sister is Lula Salt," one of the stepbrothers says. "You know her. She's in my class."

"Oh!" His eyebrows go up again.

"Actually, I have three sisters," I tell them.

"Well, you don't look much like your sisters, do you?"

"I guess not." I keep my eyes on my plate. I feel like the picked-over chicken carcass.

"Four sisters," he continues. "That's . . . unusual."

"Honey." Jason's mom lays her hand on his arm. "Why don't we let Lolly finish her dinner."

"Oh, sure." He grins at her with a mouth full

of poultry. "This is great, by the way. A meal fit for a Viking king."

She smiles at him. "I'm so glad you're enjoying it."

Later, while Mr. Bergstrom is having his after-dinner drink and Jason's mom is cleaning up the dishes, we overhear them talking. "You should be a little kinder to her, honey," Alice is saying. "She's had such a terrible time since Suzy's accident last winter. They all have. And Oren's no help. You know how he is."

Jason and I creep closer to see into the kitchen. I have my hands full with his Little League T-shirt and a container of leftovers Alice packed for me to take home, even though I told her we have plenty of food at our house.

"Of course I do. We used to be on the planning committee together. He's some kind of socialist weirdo." Mr. Bergstrom swirls his drink, and the ice cubes clink against the glass. "Of course, I don't know him as well as you do. You're the one who went out with him."

"Oh, goodness. That was thirty years ago. We were in high school." She drops an armload of dishes into the sink and turns on the faucet.

"Well, from what I hear, what happened to Suzanna wasn't exactly an accident. I never liked that woman, truth be told. She never fit in around here."

"She was troubled," Alice says. "She'd call it exhaustion, but sometimes she'd have to go into the hospital for weeks at a time. Between that and all the touring she and Oren did, the girls barely saw her. There were a few years where I practically raised them myself, and Suzy told me she thought it was better that way. She doubted her ability to be a good mother. *Singing,* she'd always say, was what she knew she was good at."

"Well, I guess it all makes sense now. *Those people.* Lots of mental health issues."

Their words turn like corkscrews in my stomach, and I wish Jason wasn't standing right there next to me, hearing it too.

"Didn't you say he met her at a bus stop or something? She was some sort of homeless person, right?"

"He saw her singing on a street corner in Portland and fell madly in love. She was barely eighteen years old, but that was that. Say what you will, she certainly was . . . talented."

Mr. Bergstrom sets his empty glass down on the counter. "Well, that only gets a person so far, Alice. You need to be strong, too. That's what I keep trying to explain to your son. There's no room for weakness in a town like this."

"Still." She opens the dishwasher. "I worry about the girls. Jason tells me Oren's hardly ever home, and they're so vulnerable up there in that house by themselves. Nobody knows if they're coming or going."

"Is that right?" He pours himself another drink. "Do they sing too?"

"What do you mean?"

"I mean like their mother. Do they also have a talent for singing?"

"Well, I don't know. It's been a while since I've seen the older girls. Why? Thinking about a part for them in the festival?"

"Maybe," he says. "We'll see."

"I'm sorry," Jason whispers.

My hands are shaking. Outside, the wind picks up and a bare branch scratches at the window. I start struggling into my jacket. "I should go home."

"Let me walk you at least."

Jason grabs a lantern from the hall closet, and we set off into the darkness of Ocean View Drive. In the off-season, the whole town shuts down after sunset, and we can't hear anything now except the occasional car going past and the waves breaking on the shore. When we were little, we always used to hold hands in the dark. But that's obviously not going to happen now. I walk on the sidewalk with my hands clutching my stuff, and Jason shuffles his sneakers along in the street, kicking at fallen leaves and swinging the lantern.

Last summer, at Jason's mom's wedding to Mr. Bergstrom, something weird happened. The wedding reception was over, and we had just waved good-bye to Alice and Mr. Bergstrom as they drove off for their honeymoon in Montreal. Everyone was yelling and cheering, and we all had these little sparklers to wave around in the darkness. Then it was time to leave, and Jason and I walked down to the dock while we waited for my parents and sisters to get their coats. There was a full moon and the air was warm, but there was a breeze blowing off the water. I was wearing one of Lily's old dresses, and the straps kept falling off my shoulders. I remember turning to Jason and saying, "It's kind of cold out." And then, suddenly, he leaned over, and he kissed me. Just like that. It landed right on the corner of my mouth. And then everybody else came outside too, and it was time to leave, and Jason and I never talked about what happened.

I don't know why I'm thinking about that now, though, as we cut across Mr. Hale's backyard and start walking up the part of Sea View Drive where the road is mostly dirt and gravel. I glance at Jason. "Did you like the chicken?"

He makes his totally disgusted face, a face reserved for things that really gross him out, like messy closets, and mayonnaise, and Mr. Bergstrom. "Are you kidding?"

I smile at the ground. Mr. Bergstrom's words are still echoing in my mind, and I want to be someplace warm and bright and safe. I want to see my dad and my sisters. "Let's stop at the diner. I'll make you an egg and cheese."

The diner stays open until midnight, but there aren't many people there on off-season weeknights this late, just my sisters. We can see them now through the window in front. They're all huddled together in the same booth, laughing and talking, and eating food off each other's plates. I don't think they would like Jason being here so late, because the Sea Witch might call, so he and I sneak around the back and in through the kitchen entrance.

"Hey, kids." Dad is scraping the grill with a spatula. There's a country song playing on the radio, and he doesn't ask me any of the normal dad questions like where I've been or if I know what time it is. I'm not sure he would know the answer to that last question himself.

"Can we make some egg and cheese sandwiches?"

"Pass me the eggs," he says. "I'll make them for you."

I'm already yanking open the heavy refrigerator door. "Thanks."

Dad fries the eggs with chopped onions and garlic and the grease from whatever else happened to be on the grill recently. He slides some extra butter onto the grill, and then he bangs the side of the spatula against it and scoops the onions into a pile. Then he slips a slice of cheddar cheese on each of the eggs. Everything is hissing and sizzling and melting, and it all smells so delicious. "So what have you guys been up to?"

"Just hanging out," Jason says.

My dad gives him a look. "That right?"

"Are you going to be at the festival, Mr. Salt?"

"Me? Of course! Suzy and I helped found that festival. Of course, back then it was all about the music. Now it's all political."

"Totally," Jason agrees, although I'm not sure he knows what my dad is talking about. I'm not sure I do either.

"Well, here you go." Dad smiles shyly as he hands us our food. "I hope these turned out okay."

I smile at him. "Thanks, Dad." *You see,* I think, *it's not that he doesn't care about being a parent. It's more like he's just never sure he's doing it right.*

We pour ourselves sodas and assemble our straws and napkins and go outside to eat at our picnic table under the pine trees. After Mr. Bergstrom's chicken, this sandwich tastes like the best thing ever. The bread is soft, the eggs are fluffy, and the cheese is perfectly warm and melted. I think that if Emma and Alice and Mr. Bergstrom could just taste these sandwiches, they'd take back every bad thing they ever said about my dad.

"I wonder what time it is," Jason says. "It must be late."

"Can I have a sip of your soda?"

"Why don't you just get your own orange soda?"

"Because I don't want that much. I just want a sip."

"Fine." He pushes it across the table.

"Are you sure?"

"It's fine."

"But are you still going to drink it after, or are you just going to dump it out?"

"I'll drink it."

"You're totally gonna dump it out."

"I won't."

"Fine." I open the plastic lid and take a sip.

"Use the straw!"

"Why?"

"You're, like, infecting the whole cup. It's full of germs right now."

I put the lid back on and push the soda across

the table, and it sits there between us. Jason looks back and forth between me and the cup for about four seconds before he grabs it and dumps it out all over the grass.

"I knew it."

Jason takes the wrapper halfway off one of the straws, and he aims it at me and blows. The wrapper flies off the straw and hits me in the face.

"Hey!" It's something we all used to do when we were kids, when we were hanging out at the diner after school, waiting for our moms. We'd started some major food fights that way.

I pull the lid off my own soda, dip my fingers inside, and pull out a dripping handful of ice cubes.

Jason jumps up and starts running, and I chase him around the table, throwing the ice. He grabs a squeeze bottle of ketchup and aims it at me.

"No!" I drop my cup, spilling the rest of the soda on the grass, and hold my hands up in surrender. "We're even!" That's what we always used to say to stop the food fights when we were kids. Those were, like, the magic words. "Even! Even! Even!"

Jason hops up on the table and sits with his legs dangling, thudding his heels against the bench.

I sit on the bench and lean my elbows on the table. "What happened to marine biology?"

"What do you mean?"

"I mean, I thought that was your dream. That's what you always wanted to do."

"I am still interested in marine biology. But I've been looking at old pictures and stuff from my real dad. Some stuff my mom keeps hidden in her closet. He was a lobsterman. And so was my grandfather. And lately I've been thinking maybe that's what I should do too. I don't know . . . that probably sounds stupid."

"No, it doesn't. It makes sense. I mean, I think it does."

"Are you sure you can't come to the dance, Lolly?"

I tilt my head up so I can see his face upside down. It's pretty dark out, but there's a thin sliver of light coming through the kitchen door, and I can hear my dad cleaning the pots. "Is Emma going?"

"Of course. She's captain of the sailing team. Why?"

I slide a little way down the bench and pick up an ice cube from the grass. "I guess she's, like, your really good friend now."

"You know, people can have more than one friend."

"But did you tell her stuff about me? I mean, did you tell her things that I said?"

"What did you say?"

"Nothing." I toss the ice as far as I can, and then I swivel back around so we can face each other. "I didn't say anything. But she said that you said that I did."

"Well, I didn't." He pokes my shoulder with his straw. "Why do you care so much about Emma?"

"Because she's mean to me. And she thinks she's better than me. And she is better than me."

"Better at what?"

I look back at him and roll my eyes. "Better at, like, everything."

He shakes his head. "But I mean, so what? Who cares?"

"I don't know. Maybe you do."

He thinks for a minute, and I keep my eyes on the sky and the way the stars stick out in these little glowing clusters between the pine trees. No clouds tonight. No storm.

"I just like hanging out with you because you're . . . you. Why do you always think that's going to change?"

Because it is going to change! All sorts of things I can't say clamor in my head. *Everything's changing!* I fold my arms across my chest and look at the ground. "I don't know."

"Why don't you come to the dance too? I mean, I want you to be there."

"Why?"

"Because I like you."

"You do?"

He tosses a wadded-up napkin at me. "I'm not saying it again."

Jason and I have been friends for a long time, but we don't normally say stuff like that to each other. I mean, of course we like each other. But we like each other because we've always just been together and we don't know any other way. Because I was there the time he got food poisoning and barfed on my bedroom rug. And because he was there when Lula gave me a really ugly haircut with bangs. Because we won a goldfish together at the town carnival by throwing Ping-Pong balls into fishbowls, and we rode together on the Cages ride that flips upside down, even though I didn't really want to. And because I was there when he got cut from the Little League team and cried. And because our parents were friends before we were ever born.

But this is different. Hearing him say that, I kind of feel happy, and I kind of want to get up and run away.

I look over at his sneakers, the ones he's worn for so long that the treads are smooth and the rubber is pulling away from the canvas. And yet they still don't have a speck of dirt on them. I would know those shoes anywhere. It is him, after all, I remind myself. He's still him. And I'm still me. Sort of. And if I go to that dance and the Sea Witch calls, well, what if I just ignore her? I mean, what's the worst that could happen? I'm not even officially a siren yet.

I pick up the napkin and toss it back at him. "Okay," I say. "I'll go."

Chapter 3

Now the Sirens have a still more fatal weapon
than their song, namely their silence.
—*Franz Kafka*

That night, I wear Jason's Little League
T-shirt to bed and sleep better than I have
in a long time, and the next day, after
school, I'm ready to serve my detention. I find Ms.
Cross back at her desk, this time reading a book,
her glasses dangling around her neck on a chain.
The classroom smells different without a bunch of
kids crowded inside, like dust and lemon soap.

"Is that new?"

She puts her glasses on and looks at me.
"What?"

"The chain. I've never seen it before."

"Oh," she says. "Yes. It was a gift."

"That's a good gift for you," I tell her. "I mean, you take your glasses on and off a lot."

"Yes," she says. "Well." She opens the bottom drawer of her desk, pulls out some whiteboard cleaner and a roll of paper towels, and hands them to me. "Here you are, dear. You can clean the whiteboard."

The notes from the day's classes are still up, messy and smeared in places where kids' backpacks rubbed against them: Salem, 1654, perspective, critical thinking, fairness. I spray the cleaning solution, trying not to breathe it in, and pull a few paper towels off the roll.

"You don't like history," Ms. Cross says suddenly.

I look at her over my shoulder, but she's still looking down at her book.

"At least that's what your tardiness and skipping seem to suggest."

"I do like history," I tell her. "There are just some things about this class that bother me."

She plucks a pen from the mug on her desk and starts chewing on the cap. "Like what?" Nobody likes borrowing pens from Ms. Cross because they're all covered in little bite marks.

I turn back to the board and spray some more cleaning solution. "I don't know."

"I think you do," she says. "And I'll tell you something else, I'm not letting you off the hook so easily this time. I'd like to hear what you have to *say* for once instead of just watching you scowl at me from the back row."

Picturing myself from Ms. Cross's perspective is alarming. I guess it's like when customers complain about us at the diner while we're standing right there in front of them. It's like they think as long as we're behind the counter, we can't hear them. Like we're invisible.

"I don't mean to scowl at you."

"Well, go on, then. Let's hear what you've been thinking about all this time."

There's so much I could tell her. I've been thinking about shipwrecks and losing my best friend. I've been thinking about my mom. "I don't like our textbook," I tell her. "*The American Vision* or whatever. I don't—I don't feel like I'm included in the vision."

"What do you mean?"

"Well, my mom was born on the reservation near Old Town, not too far from here, but we never learn anything about that." I glance at her. "In fact, there's nothing about reservations in the textbook at all."

"I see." Ms. Cross nods and folds her hands on the desk. "That is . . . true. I'm sorry about that, Lorelei."

She's never called me by my first name before.

I look around the room, at the lanterns and the cupboards and the sink in the corner that's always leaking. Before Starbridge Cove was made part of the Sunrise County school district, this room used to be a chemistry lab. But then a whole new science wing got added on, and now Ms. Cross just uses the sink to make tea. She has an electric kettle and an assortment of multicolored teacups hanging on hooks above the counter. I like that none of them match. I know my mom would like it too.

I stand on my toes and start cleaning the top corner of the board. "My mom didn't talk much about her family, so I don't know a lot about them either. But I want to."

"You never met them?"

"No. She was taken from her home when she was little, put in foster care on the mainland, and then she ran away from there when she turned sixteen."

"And she never tried to go back? To her parents?"

"I don't think so. My sisters say she felt ashamed and out of place, like she didn't quite belong in either setting. Like, she was an outsider wherever she went, you know?"

Ms. Cross takes her glasses off and starts cleaning the lenses with her scarf. "I do."

"My sisters say a lot of bad things happened to her biological parents too. And their parents. And their parents' parents. They say there were just so many layers of sadness, it was like they couldn't get out from under them all."

Ms. Cross is quiet for a moment, and then she clears her throat and gets up from the desk. "Excuse me for a moment, would you?" She takes a plastic spray bottle from under the sink and walks to the tangle of assorted plants on the windowsill. "I'm noticing now that some of these are in dire straits."

With her back to me, Ms. Cross plucks a few dead leaves and crumples them in her palm, and then she checks on the others, lifting individual leaves before misting more water on each plant. "Yes," she says, and I'm not exactly sure if she's addressing me or the azaleas. "It's a real—it's an awful mess, isn't it? It's hard to look too closely sometimes. One starts to see how bad a situation really is."

I turn back to cleaning the whiteboard, and for a while, all you can hear in the room is the two of us spraying and tidying. The four o'clock sunlight starts to spill like syrup through the smudges on the windowpanes.

Then the bell rings, and we both jump. "Goodness." Ms. Cross shakes her head and mists her spray bottle at the loudspeaker. "That bell is an act of violence."

She sets the bottle down by the sink and starts washing her hands.

I pass her a paper towel.

"Look, it's almost time for you to go home now, but, speaking of music, there's something I'd like to show you."

With surprisingly good aim, Ms. Cross tosses her crumpled paper towel into the wastepaper basket, and then she goes to the little shelf behind her desk, where she keeps what I've always assumed are her really important books. She runs her fingers over the spines. "Aha! Here we are." She holds the book above her head for a moment and then places it faceup on the table. "Why don't you have a seat?"

I take a seat.

Sure enough, this is no ordinary textbook.

This book is bound in leather, stamped in gold, and handwritten. Intricate maps, odd symbols, and detailed illustrations crowd the margins.

Ms. Cross turns a few pages and stops at a pen-and-ink drawing of a girl with long wavy hair and feet like a bird's.

The Seiren of Starbridge Cove

Oh no, I think.

"Lorelei," she says. "I have to ask you something."

"What?" I'm already climbing out of the chair.

"Are you one of them?"

"One of what?"

"Don't be afraid," she says. "It's just that I've worked at this school for a long time, and I believe I can spot a girl who's becoming a siren. They are the restless ones, the ones with their hands pulled into their sleeves and their hair in tangles. Dark circles under their eyes. You are not the first. On the contrary. I once knew a whole group of girls like you. Girls who disappeared."

"What are you talking about?"

"I mean, they started out like you, skipping class, showing up late, always losing things. Meanwhile, there was an increase in violent storms, strange weather—tornadoes one day and hurricanes the next. And shipwrecks. Terrible shipwrecks. Several people lost their lives. And then, one day, the girls all disappeared. The storms stopped, and the whole town seemed to forget."

"Their own families forgot about them?"

"Well, there was a group home here in town, a sort of orphanage, although I don't care much for that term. Most of the girls came from there. But the home was shut down years ago, and I haven't seen any others like them since. I've been thinking about them all this time, though. Wondering what happened."

"But how did you know—I mean, why did you think they were sirens?"

"One can't live in Starbridge Cove long without knowing something of the old siren lore. You know that. I discovered this diary years ago, doing my graduate research on the trial of Hannah Martin. I believe it belonged if not to Hannah herself, then to a woman who experienced a similar ordeal." She points to the book. "Many of the entries mention sirens, and I always suspected that they were real. I thought of it again when those girls disappeared. And then you showed up in my class this year, and you just . . . well, you seemed so much like they did."

I shake my head, but there are tears burning behind my eyes. "I'm sorry," I tell her. "I don't know what you're talking about."

"I see." She looks away. "Well, nevertheless, borrow the journal, Lorelei. Please. I'd like you to read it."

I tuck the book carefully under my arm and look up at the clock. "I think it's time to go."

"You know, often it's guilt that makes people act in a way they shouldn't. Or not want to face the things they should."

"Have a good night," I tell her, and pull the door shut behind me.

That night, I curl up in Lara's bed with a flashlight and Hannah's journal. Lara's already fallen asleep, with her golden hair spread across the pillow and her arms flung above her head. She always sleeps sprawled out like that, like she doesn't have a care in the world. Lily and Lula are downstairs with some kids from school, but they'll be kicking them out soon, before it gets too late. Nobody is ever allowed to stay.

I want to tell them everything Ms. Cross said, about the journal and the girls who disappeared, about Mr. Bergstrom and how he asked Alice about us. But I'm sure they'll just tell me to stop worrying again. They'll tell me we're more powerful than anything now, and that we don't have to be scared anymore. Not as long as we're together.

June 28th, 1694

It is a witch they want, and it is a witch they believe they have captured. Well, if this works, this dark magic, they will come for me in the morning, and there will not be anybody here resembling the terrified young girl they locked in this cell two nights ago. Her soul will have flown free through the bars on the windows, and she will look down on this town as birds do, on the prisons, and the graveyard, and the harbor, and the ships. And she will hide away, in that distant land beyond the horizon, between the ocean and the stars. And here, in this cell, they will find only what remains: a woman changed, stronger than before, more powerful, and accompanied by a starving wolf. They will have their witch. And they will not have the courage to hang her, no matter what the witness says.

With shaking fingers, I turn the pages until I get to a part near the end, the part about sirens.

The new seirens seem frightened by their power and changes to their physical appearance. At night, they cry themselves to sleep. I suppose it's only normal for a girl to wish she could go back in time and reverse the spell that changed her from an ordinary child into an otherworldly temptress.

Yes, I think. *Exactly.*

The diary continues:

But wishing for such things is foolish and a waste of energy. Reversal of a seiren spell is, in most cases, impossible. Soon they will abandon all hope and accept their fate as protectors of the sea, for their souls are not their own.

Beside me, Lara murmurs something and rolls over in her sleep, and I shut the book and set it back down on the floor. I feel like throwing it across the room. Instead, I tuck my knees up to my chest and wrap my arms around them to keep warm. Through the half-open window, I can hear Lily laughing, and the wind, and the melancholy music of another folk troupe rehearsing in the moonlight on the outdoor stage.

† † †

The rest of the week passes in a blur. Even more of
a blur than usual. Dad switches the diner over to
the winter menu, which involves more chowders
and comfort foods like chili and macaroni and
cheese. The Sea Witch calls for us at two o'clock
one morning and we wreck another trawler. In
English class we read an excerpt from *Macbeth* and
the main character tells us that his mind is filled
with scorpions. *Me too,* I think. My mind is filled
with scorpions. I'm afraid of becoming a siren,
and I'm afraid that Mr. Bergstrom is going to make
us disappear like the girls in Ms. Cross's story, and
secretly, even though I know it's not the same, I'm
afraid of the promise I made to Jason. I'm afraid of
attending my first middle school dance.

Friday afternoon I spend about three hours
walking back and forth between all our closets and
the full-length mirror in the hallway, trying different outfits. At last I settle on silver sandals and
a floaty sea-foam dress that Lula wore to her first
prom, a prom she attended while still in eighth
grade. At the time, Lula's prom debut was like the
small-town scandal of the century. Our mom used

to complain that she couldn't even get down the aisle at the supermarket without people whispering about her parenting skills and "the sort of girls" she was raising. But then, our mom didn't spend much time at the supermarket anyway.

I twist my hair up into a knot so the platinum streaks won't show, and then I use some of Lily's lipstick and blush that I assume is the right shade. Finally, I pack Lara's silver purse with all of my makeup and a nail file, just in case, and head downstairs.

My sisters are sitting at the kitchen table, drinking Lara's famous spiced hot chocolate from the mismatched seashell mugs and playing cards. Lula is sitting with her legs tucked underneath her, studying her cards and drumming her perfectly manicured nails on the tabletop. Lily has her bare feet up on the table, and I can see her turquoise scales shining in the light. I cross my fingers and hope they won't see me. Maybe I can just sneak right out the door. But that's impossible with Lara around. She has some sort of sixth sense where all of us are concerned.

Sure enough, Lara sees me standing in the

doorway and sets down her cards. "Lolly? It's late. Why are you all dressed up? Where are you going?"

"To see Dad."

"In that dress?"

Lily leans forward. "Are you wearing makeup?"

"Doesn't he have a gig tonight?"

"Yeah, but he invited me."

"We were going to watch a movie on TV, *Woman on the Run*."

I'm a woman on the run. "I don't know, Lara. I promised Dad."

"If she calls for us tonight—" Lula starts.

Lily finishes the sentence for her. "You're going to be in big trouble."

I shake my head. "She never calls us before midnight. Those cargo ships always come into port at, like, four in the morning."

Lula shrugs. "That's true. And even if she did call, Dad probably wouldn't notice."

Lily looks at my feet. "You're wearing sandals?"

"Yeah. So?"

"So I think I can see your scales."

I look down. "Not really. I mean, you barely can. Plus, it's gonna be dark."

"Well, enjoy it while you can. They're going to grow longer soon." She wiggles her toes. "Like mine."

"Okay, Lily. But not right this second. So just leave me alone."

Lily raises her eyebrows. "Ew."

"All right, little lady." Lara picks up her cards. "Go see Dad. But be careful."

"I will."

"And take a coat!"

Our house is one of the oldest in Starbridge Cove, and we don't have a view of the ocean or private beach access like Emma and Jason. But we can still hear the ocean, the waves breaking on the rocks, and the seagulls; and the air has the same smell of pine needles and salt. I walk the long gravel drive that connects our house to the diner, keeping my arms wrapped tightly over my chest because the nights are already getting cold and I didn't listen to Lara and take a coat.

Our driveway is lined on either side by a dense pine forest, and it floods every time it rains. I used to hate getting rides from people because nobody

ever believed we actually live here. "Are you sure
this is the driveway, Lolly?" they'd always ask. "Is it
possible you've got the directions wrong?" We kept
asking Dad to pave the road and install more lights
but he kept on forgetting. Of course, now that I
don't do gymnastics anymore, I don't ever need
rides from people anyway, so, as Ms. Cross always
says, "the point is moot."

The driveway winds all the way downhill and
ends at Seawall Avenue. From there you can see
the ocean, and the diner is just ahead. Dad has the
light on in the apartment upstairs, and I recognize
his silhouette through the window. He should
probably get himself some curtains, but maybe
that would be too much like admitting he actually
lives there.

Contrary to what Emma thinks, Dad didn't just
wake up one morning, decide he was too cool for
us, and move out of our house. What really happened is that he slowly detached and peeled himself away, much like an octopus I once saw in one
of Jason's documentaries. I'm not sure Dad himself was even fully aware of what was going on.
First, he moved out of his bedroom and down the

hall to the guest room. We probably wouldn't have even noticed except that his snoring normally woke Lula, whose bedroom was on the other side of the wall.

Weeks later, he migrated downstairs, setting up camp on the floor in the study. I happened to go in there one afternoon in search of extra high-lighters, and I spotted his blankets and sheets, all neatly folded, in an orderly pile on top of the fully inflated air mattress. Gradually, more and more of his stuff began to leave with him in the morn-ings and not come back. Music he wanted to play while he was cooking. Sweaters. Books. His guitar. The first time Dad left with his overnight bag, we watched him go.

"I'll be staying right down the road," he assured us, slinging the duffel bag over his shoulder. Nobody was saying it out loud, but I think it had occurred to all of us by then that if he was capable of migrating this far, there was no telling where he might go. With our mom's death, it was like all the normal boundaries and obstacles that come with being a family were gone, and Dad was unmoored, skating away with nothing to stop him, like the objects in chapter 7 of our science textbook, *The Wondrous Capabilities of a Frictionless Surface.*

"I'll see you at the diner every day," he continued. "Okay? So it'll be like I'm not even really gone. And if you need anything, you just call or come on over. Right? You'll barely even miss me."

"Right." All I could see was the illustration of a giant piano sliding across a skating rink.

"Who's gonna do the laundry?" Lily asked. Even when Mom was alive, Dad was the one who did most of the housework.

Lara said, "I think we'll manage." Then she and Lula said good-bye and went back into the kitchen and started making dinner like nothing weird was going on. Or rather, Lara started making dinner and Lula helped the way she always did, by sitting at the kitchen table and changing her nail polish for the fourth time that week.

But Lily and I watched. We stood in the window, close enough together that our shoulders were touching, and we watched him head off into the sunset like he was starring in his own cowboy movie.

"Do you think it's our fault?" Lily asked.

I shrugged. "Maybe."

I think we were both recalling all the times over the last few months when we'd been difficult to live with. Tired. Distant. Secretive. I guess a dad can't be expected to notice or understand when his daughters start turning into sirens. I barely understood it myself. All my sisters would ever tell me was that they'd made a deal with the Sea Witch and that I was a part of it, that it meant we were all going to be more beautiful and more powerful than we ever could have dreamed, and that we'd live that way forever. We had just lost our mother, and it made sense to me somehow that they'd make a deal like that. When you lose someone you love, for a while it's like there's this strange, shimmering cloud around you and your family. The loss is so powerful, it's almost magic. Like you've fallen through a secret portal or seen into another world. Anything could happen. But they would never tell me why or how it happened to them. Lara just promised I'd find out when I was older, when my own transformation was complete. And if they weren't going to explain it to me, they certainly weren't going to explain it to Dad.

He was leaving us his truck, and some of his

flannel shirts, which we'd end up wearing as nightgowns, and the pistol he kept for protection from bears. Bears are pretty common around here, but they usually keep to themselves. They don't really bother anybody. But Dad would insist he could hear them at night, prowling around in the woods behind our house. He claimed they weren't like ordinary black bears either, that they were bigger than normal and that their fur was white. "Ghost bears," he kept calling them. "Some type of albino or something."

Jason told me it was possible, that there was such a thing as a Kermode or spirit bear, and they made up just one percent of the black bear population. He said it was an extremely rare genetic mutation, though, one never seen before in this region (even though we have tons of regular bears), and that if there were Kermode living in our very own woods, it would be a true wonder of science. In any case, Dad hates guns, and he certainly had no interest in hunting, so he kept the pistol loaded with blanks, figuring that if one of the ghost bears ever got too close, he'd just fire and scare it away with the sound.

"Remember to keep the garbage cans locked up tight, girls." That was the last thing he said, right before he slipped out the door.

I come in through the kitchen and walk up the back steps. At the apartment now, Dad has three guitars, two pairs of boots, an old wood-burning stove, and a couch with a colorful blanket draped over it. But mostly he has cassette tapes, boxes and boxes of them that he keeps in crates all over the floor. There are tapestries nailed to the wall, and a black-and-white photograph of him and my mom together onstage at a concert. In the picture, my mom is in profile, holding her guitar, with her dark hair falling over her face and her eyes cast down at the floor. She's wearing some kind of gauzy tunic with flowers embroidered around the collar. Beneath the bright lights, she looks like an angel.

"Hey, kid." Dad's standing at the sink rinsing out a coffee cup. He smiles at me and his eyes crinkle behind his glasses. "I'm glad you came." He always greets me like this, like we're long-lost friends and he can't believe he's seeing me again after all these years, even though it's only been, like, eight hours.

"You ready to go?"

He nods. "Just about. But listen, Lolly, there's something I wanted to ask you first."

"Sure. Is everything all right?"

He sits down on an overturned crate and takes my hands in his. "Well, I'm thinking about going out on tour again."

I pull my hands away and take a step backward. "What?"

"I have a buddy who's playing over in Boston right now and then touring out west next month. I was thinking I could meet up with him this week and see how it goes."

"This week?"

"Well, yes. Immediately."

"But what about the festival?"

"Well, I'd have to miss it. I'd be leaving tomorrow. But it's a great opportunity, Lolly. And I'd be back in a few days. What do you think?"

I think again about the speeding piano demonstration, the illustration they don't include where the piano eventually crashes against the wall of the skating rink and smashes into a million pieces. "Did Jason's mom say something to you?"

"Alice? About what? What would she say?"

"About not being a good parent or something. Because it's not true, you know. You're a good— well, you're doing fine." I keep remembering when I was little and he and my mom were getting ready to go out on tour. I'd have a tantrum and throw myself at his feet and wrap my arms around his legs to keep him from leaving. "Don't let her scare you away. Okay? We still need you here."

"She's not scaring me away, Lolly. This has nothing to do with Alice. This is about me. The truth is, I haven't been feeling too well lately, and I thought maybe getting out of town for a few days . . . well, I thought maybe it would do me some good."

I look down at my sandals. One tiny iridescent scale peeks out from beneath the silver straps. "I guess if it's a good opportunity, then you should do it."

"Well, that's what I think too. But I wanted to make sure you'd be okay with it."

"Is everyone else okay with it? I mean, did you ask Lara?"

"They'll be fine. But you know, they're . . . older than you."

"Well, I'm fine with it too."

"Okay, then." He nods. "I guess I forget sometimes you're not a little kid anymore. I still picture you having temper tantrums and getting upset every time we leave the house."

"Right." I'm still seeing the speeding piano in my head, only now I have an urge to shove him in front of it.

"Well, thanks for being so cool about it, kid. And we'll celebrate your birthday together when I get back. Okay? Don't think I forgot."

"Sure. No problem."

"Okay, let's get this show on the road." He takes his guitar in one hand and my hand in the other, and we make our way back down the stairs to the kitchen.

I barely recognize the diner. The place is transformed in semidarkness, with twinkle lights around the windows and mirror balls twirling overhead, bathing the audience in a million tiny circles of light. It's so beautiful that I almost forget to be angry at Dad. The band starts up their new song, "On the Ghost Road," and I watch the people in the audience. To my surprise, Alice is there, sitting alone in the back with her chin resting on her hands. She looks like she's on the verge of tears. When it's good, that's the kind of thing music can do. That's what our mom always used to say. *That's the kind of power it has.*

Years ago, when our parents went on tour together, we'd stay over at Jason's and sleep in sleeping bags on the floor or, if the weather was warm, outside in the field behind their trailer. Alice would make pancakes for dinner, and Lula would drink maple syrup straight out of a juice glass, and Lara would let me play with her makeup and French-braid my hair to distract me from being homesick. Then we'd stay up late to listen to their interviews and live performances on the radio, like transmissions from outer space. I remember listening for the sound of Mom's voice before it got swallowed up in static, and I remember feeling sleepy and wide awake at the same time, and the rush from the sugar and having my hair pulled back too tight.

But Dad stopped touring completely when Mom

died. Since the accident, he hasn't even left Starbridge Cove. So maybe he's right. Maybe this trip will be good for him. And we're not little kids anymore. I guess we can take care of ourselves now.

At the end of the first set, I catch Dad's eye and give him a small wave. It's time. I'm a woman on the run.

Dad nods, and I start snaking my way back through the little tables, trying not to disturb anyone or bang into anything.

And then I smack straight into the Sea Witch.

She's standing by the open door with her wild gray hair blowing crazily in the breeze. She's nearly six feet tall and is wearing chandelier earrings and a sparkly dress. People are staring at her, but I can't tell if she realizes it. Or if, like my sisters, she's perfected the art of attracting attention without letting it concern her. She's smoking a cigarette, and she has one hand on her hip and a shawl thrown over her shoulders like an old movie star, like she's posing in some kind of weird sea witch fashion magazine.

"What are you doing here?"

The Sea Witch almost never visits the

mainland. And when she does, she never goes far-ther than the beach. Seeing her all dressed up and out at a concert is as weird as when Nurse Claire started showing up at the diner on Sundays on the back of Coach Bouchard's motorcycle. Or the time I saw Ms. Cross in the produce section at the supermarket choosing an avocado.

The Sea Witch smiles. "Didn't you know, Lolly? I am a great patron of the arts."

"You shouldn't smoke," I tell her. "It's really bad for you."

"Ha!" She gestures dramatically with her ciga-rette, leaving smoke trails in the air. "Mortality is the least of my concerns, dear. Yours as well, come to think of it."

"I have to go."

She sniffs the air. "You smell like perfume."

"I'm already late."

"For what? Where are you going?"

She knows. I can hear it in her voice. She knows everything about us. "Home," I tell her. "I'm going home."

The Sea Witch laughs. "So this is your big idea? You think you're just going to ignore me and carry on living your life like a normal girl? Go to dances? Make *friends*?"

I put my hands on my hips. "What if I do?"

"Lorelei, I hate to rain on your parade, but no sailor in this town is safe from my sirens. Now, everyone in this town is a sailor of one sort or another, and in two days' time, you will be one of my sirens. Ergo, no one in this town is safe from you. You can attend all the dances you like, but you cannot shut your eyes and pretend this isn't happening. This is a powerful magic. Even I struggle occasionally to control it. Soon it will transform you into a cold-blooded monster, and the more attachments you have with other people when the transformation occurs, the harder it will be."

"Well, maybe I'm willing to take that risk."

"Then go if you want. Live in denial for one more day. You certainly wouldn't be the first. But trust me, dear, sirens make terrible friends."

I push past her and run out to the parking lot and across the street to catch the bus. I keep look-ing back over my shoulder to make sure she isn't following me. The bus stop is right by the

Dumpsters, and the air smells like seawater and rotten fish. I cross my arms over my chest and tap my feet, muttering under my breath. "Hurry up. Hurry up!"

At last, the bus comes chugging into view. The doors swing open, and I grab the railing and pull myself up into the cold, stale air. As we speed down Seawall Avenue, I look out the window and try to think of a plan. Maybe Jason and I could run away, leave Starbridge Cove and go someplace else, someplace the Sea Witch would never find me, someplace far from the ocean where there's no such thing as shipwrecks. Like a desert. Or the top of a mountain. And if my sisters like being sirens so much, then they can just stay here and be as cold-blooded and beautiful as they want. They can do it without me.

It's totally weird being in the gym after dark. The lights are low, and there are streamers and paper stars hanging from the basketball hoop. There's music playing but nobody's dancing. Instead, kids are roaming the floor in packs. The gymnastics girls are all wearing the same gold sandals and pink bows in their hair. Jason is sitting by the refreshment table with the entire sailing team, but I'm too scared to go over uninvited. Meanwhile, Emma floats effortlessly between the two groups. She belongs everywhere.

I lean against the wall across from the bleachers and glance at the clock. What if Jason changed his mind about wanting me here? What if nobody ever talks to me? What if I just stand here all night long?

But then Jason turns around and sees me, and he smiles and starts waving me over. I can't believe it. The entire sailing team is watching.

I take a deep breath and push myself away from the wall.

"Hey," he says. "You made it."

I grab a cup of soda from the refreshment table and hold on tight like it's the only thing keeping me from falling through the floor. "Yeah," I say. "I'm here."

"I'm so embarrassed."

"You are? Why?"

"At the last minute, my stepdad decided to insist on being a chaperone." He points to the speakers, where Mr. Bergstrom is talking to Coach Bouchard. We can't hear him over the music, but we can see that he's upset; he's gesturing wildly with his hands. Coach Bouchard keeps nodding and trying to back away at the same time. "It's not like he's here because he wanted to spend time with me either. He just wanted to 'share some ideas' with Coach Bouchard about the festival. And by 'share some ideas' he means yell at him and demand that he do everything his way."

"I'm sorry."

"Well, I'm just glad you're here. I like your necklace."

"Thanks. I, um, I wear it every day."

"Oh. Well, it looks good today." He flips a pretzel in the air and catches it in his mouth, the way his stepbrothers always do. I can't believe he's coordinated enough to pull off a maneuver like that at a time like this.

"You seem very . . . relaxed."

"What does that mean?"

"I don't know."

Thankfully, before I can say any more weird things, the music changes to a slow song, and it's like this invisible tide, swirling people into couples and dragging them out to the dance floor. Even Coach Bouchard and Nurse Claire get swept out into the crowd and start dancing with each other.

"So?" Jason asks. "Do you want to dance?"

"With you?"

"I mean, yeah."

"Sure."

We drift out to the dance floor and find a place for ourselves in the crowd. He puts his hands on my waist, and I put my hands on his shoulders. We're still about the same height, so it's hard to avoid eye contact. But we try. We look everywhere around the room except at each other: at the basketball hoop, and the paper stars, and the refreshment table. His neck is turning red, and his hands are sweating through my dress. It's a little gross. Still, for the next ninety seconds, we are like two totally normal kids at a middle school dance, and I kind of can't believe it. Soon, I think, I'll tell him my idea about running away. We'll devise a plan and pool our resources. He'll have some ideas about useful tools for surviving in the wilderness, like maps or rope or whatever. I'll pack us some food from the diner, like peanut butter, which lasts a really long time, and my books, and we'll take all of the snacks from his room, and—

And then the power goes out.

"It's the storm!"

"Get away from the windows!"

The chaperones start trying to corral us all into the center of the gym, and someone starts the backup generator. The smell of gasoline fills the room, and the gym is flooded with yellow light.

A tingling sensation shivers through my feet and ankles.

Jason tries to grab my arm, but I pull away from him and run for the bathroom as fast as I can. I lock myself in a stall and sit on the floor with my knees drawn up to my chest. Scales are now twining their way over my feet and up my ankles like vines. Like snakes. I hug my knees tight and try not to cry.

Under the fluorescent lights, my feet don't even look like mine anymore. They look like alligator feet. It's totally disgusting, and I grab the nail file from my purse and start scraping my ankles with the rough side as hard as I can. Scales fall away and land in a shimmering pile on the floor, but more immediately grow back in their place. It's hopeless. I can't stop them anymore.

Outside, I hear thunder, and hail pings against the window. The storm is getting worse, and I need to leave. This was all a terrible idea. Lily was right. I never should have worn these shoes. I never should have come here. And I never should have even thought of running away. The Sea Witch could cause a hurricane to get back at me. A tornado. She could destroy our house and the school and the diner. She could destroy the whole town.

I wipe my face with the back of my hand, and I scoop up my scales and throw them in the garbage. And then I take the silver sandals and shove them into the garbage too. Trembling, I scramble up onto the counter, push open the window, and climb outside into the pouring rain.

I take off running across the parking lot, the silver purse banging against my hip, trying not to slip in the mud while the rain soaks my hair and Lula's dress, and hail pelts my face and arms like it's meant especially for me. For just one second,

I glance back at the school, and I see Mr. Bergstrom standing by the main entrance wearing a green poncho and holding a flashlight. He points the flashlight at me and starts waving me over. "Lorelei Salt! I see you! Come back here!" But I keep running as fast as I can into the darkness.

The next morning, I wake up curled in Lara's bed. I'm still wearing Lula's dress, which is like a cold, wet skin, and my arms and legs are streaked with mud. For a while I just lie there, staring up at the headboard with its pattern of smooth metal bars. My sisters are all awake, and the smell of coffee and bacon and the sound of their voices, laughing and teasing, float up from the kitchen. But outside, below my window, there're these strange banging and rustling sounds.

I peel off Lula's dress and grab Jason's Little League T-shirt from the back of a chair. I pull the shirt on over my head and go look outside. Two stories below, a figure stands hunched over the trash cans, pawing through bottles and newspapers, a dark, hulking shape in the foggy gray morning. At first I think it's one of Dad's mythical ghost bears. But then the figure straightens and pushes back his hood, and I recognize him. It's Mr. Bergstrom. His hair is all messed up, and his eyes are wild, and he has a series of rust-colored stains sprayed across the sleeves of his jacket.

I'm just as afraid as when I thought it was a bear.

I back away from the window and hurry across the cold floorboards and down the stairs.

"Lara!"

"What is it?" She comes into the hall holding a wooden spoon, cheeks flushed from standing over the stove. "I was just coming to wake you. I made oatmeal."

"I have to tell you something."

"You're shaking, Lolly. What's wrong?" She comes closer and rubs my arms. "Bad dream?"

"Lara, I went to a dance last night."

"A dance?"

"Yes. At school. I lied to you."

She grins. "I think you can be forgiven for that."

"But that's not the worst part. I ran away because the power went out, because the Sea Witch was calling, and Mr. Bergstrom saw me. He saw me running away, and I think he knows something. About us. I told you he's hunted sirens before, and that he said he knows how to spot them."

"Okay, well, it's good you told me. I'll just—"

"No, but there's more."

"What do you mean?"

"I mean he's outside right now. By the garbage cans. He's here. At our house."

There's a pounding on the door then, hard enough to shake the rusty dead bolt and rattle the pictures on the walls.

Lara grabs my elbow and pulls me to her side. "Lula! Come in here!"

The pounding gets louder, and Lula and Lily both come into the hallway in their pajamas and socks. Lula's still holding a bowl of oatmeal. "What's all that banging? What's going on?"

"Erik Bergstrom is outside. I'm going to go talk to him. Just take them down to the basement in case— Well, Dad's gun is there."

"It doesn't have any bullets!" Lily reminds everyone.

Lara puts her finger to her lips. Then she

opens the front door and steps out onto the porch, and the three of us ignore her instructions and hide in the living room where we can see everything through the window.

"Can I help you?" Lara can ask that question like the wrong answer might get your head chopped off, but Mr. Bergstrom doesn't seem concerned.

"Where's your father?"

"He isn't home. What is this regarding?"

"What is this regarding? It's regarding your little sister. She ran away from an official school function last night, in the middle of the storm. I'd like to know where she thought she was going."

I can feel Lily glaring at me, but I refuse to look at her.

"How is that any of your business?"

"I was an official chaperone at the function," he explains. "So that gives me jurisdiction."

"I see. Well, she's here now. She's fine. Thank you for . . . following up. Now I'd like you to leave."

"Or else what?"

"Or I'm calling the police."

"The police?" We can hear Mr. Bergstrom

laugh and then his steps on the porch stairs. "Why do you think this town even *has* a police force? I'm the biggest donor and fund-raiser in Sunrise County. I own the police."

Even from this distance, I can tell Lara's a little scared now. She keeps biting her lip and raking her hands through her hair, and I think she looks a lot smaller, too, without the rest of us around her.

"What about you, young lady? Pretty bad storm we had last night. Where were you?"

"Leave us alone."

"You know I'm a hunter, right?"

Lara shakes her head. "I don't know you at all."

Mr. Bergstrom raises his eyebrows. "Well, let me tell you something about me, then. I'm a developer by trade, okay? A visionary. I have a vision for a place, and then I eliminate all the obstacles in my way. You understand? Hunting is just a part of that."

He takes another step, and Lily and I scoot closer together and push the curtain aside to see. Now Mr. Bergstrom has one palm braced against the wall and he's leaning close to Lara's face. "I

don't care how fearsome a creature seems, how big
it is, what it's capable of. If it's in my way, it'll be
hanging on my wall by dinnertime."

Lula starts trying to stand up, but she slips in
her socks, and Lily grabs her hand and pulls her
back down. "Wait," she hisses. "He's leaving."

Mr. Bergstrom turns and walks back out to his
truck, and Lara comes inside and shuts the door.
The three of us trip over each other trying to get
back to her.

"Let's go downstairs," she says. "Family meeting."

We all head down to the basement, which is a
place I don't really like going to anymore. It smells
like mold and cobwebs, and it's full of cardboard
boxes and our mom's old records and clothes.

"He obviously knows about us," Lily says, and
points at me. "Thanks to her."

"It's not my fault. He already knew!" I say.

"What are you talking about?"

"I heard him at the diner telling Mr. Bishop
that he knows sirens are real. That he can spot
them and that he's hunted them before."

"Well, why didn't you tell us, then?"

"I tried! I told Lara, but she—"

Lara sighs and pushes her bangs out of her face. "She did. I didn't listen to her."

For a while nobody says anything. Then Lula pulls the spoon out of her oatmeal and frowns at the hardened clumps. "I can't eat this now."

"Look," Lara says. "Somebody just has to go explain all of this to the Sea Witch. She shouldn't call for us for a while. Just in case. It's too dangerous."

Lily calls out, "Not it!" and puts her finger on her nose, which is supposed to be like some sort of guaranteed protection against anyone ever making her do anything. It's the same way she always calls the window seat in the truck; then nobody can ever make her smush in the middle.

I'm always in the middle.

I raise my hand. "I'll go."

Lara smiles. "That's very brave of you, Lolly. Thank you."

Lily rolls her eyes. "It's about time she did something useful."

By the time I leave the basement, thick gray storm clouds are gathering overhead. This time, I manage to extricate my own bottle-green raincoat and rubber boots from the mess of the hall closet, and I slosh out into the misty morning. Aside from a trail of heavy boot prints in the mud, there's no sign of Mr. Bergstrom, and I walk alone until the shoreline comes into view and then head down to the dock where we keep our family's kayak.

Practically every family in Starbridge Cove has some sort of kayak, and by the time they're nine or ten, most kids can pilot one all on their own. I climb into the little boat, take a seat on one of the benches, and slide the paddle into my hands. The little vessel tips and sways a bit, and I try to steady myself, to keep my balance. Once I'm settled and I start paddling in a steady rhythm, the vessel moves quickly across the inlet, gliding, as if the water were glass. The Sea Witch's house comes into view, a rickety old cottage in the center of a tiny island, barely big enough for the house and a large rock and three scrawny trees, and it occurs to me that I've never actually been there before by myself.

I dip the paddle into the water to slow down, and I guide the kayak into a space by her dock. I

drag the boat up onto the shore and leave it overturned with the paddle inside. Then I approach
the front porch. I duck beneath the wind chimes,
made of feather and bone, and knock at the door.

"Just a second!" The Sea Witch has terrible
eyesight, but she can smell human flesh from
miles away; she probably already knows that it's
me. Still, she opens the door a crack and pokes her
nose out and sniffs the air to be sure. Then she
lets the door swing wide. "Lorelei! What a lovely
surprise." She winks. "How was your evening?"

I roll my eyes and step past her into the musty
little kitchen.

She sniffs the air again. "It's dark in here, isn't
it? Excuse me for a moment. There's tea on the
table. You may help yourself."

The room is so cluttered, there's barely space to
move. In the growing darkness, I can see all of her
treasures—the spinning wheels, the nets, buoys,
telescopes, treasure boxes, and statues, everything
she's stolen from shipwrecks over the years—stacked
in the corners and suspended from the ceiling.
Some of the items she sells at flea markets and fancy
antique shops. Others she uses in her spells.

There's a low growling sound, and her monstrous pet wolf comes lumbering out of the shadows. I hold my breath and try not to move, but he comes right over and starts licking my arms, slobbering all over my boots.

"There we are!" The Sea Witch sweeps back into the room with a lighted candle and sits at the table, wrapped in her glamorous, sea witch movie-star shawl. The wolf lies flat at her feet. "Sit, dear. Please." She pours us each a cup of tea. "Now, tell me, what brings you here today?"

"My sisters sent me. They want you to know that you can't call for us for a while. We need a break."

"A break?" The Sea Witch makes a face as if she's just smelled something hideous. "This isn't some sort of part-time job, you know."

"Yes, but we're scared. We think someone in town, someone powerful, knows what we are. We think he's trying to protect the harbor from us."

"*I'm* protecting the harbor," she says. "From him."

"Well, he doesn't see it that way."

The Sea Witch sips her tea. "I'm sorry, Lolly,

but this is unacceptable. What if I need you?"

I try to make my voice sound strong, like Lara's, but it's hard to argue with her now. I've seen what she's capable of. "We just don't think it's a good idea."

"Well, my dear, it isn't up to you. Nor is it up to your sisters. In fact, it's barely up to me. This is in the hands of a magic that's bigger than all of us. But your sisters signed on fair and square. They knew the deal."

I trace my finger over a place in the table where somebody carved a set of initials in a heart shape. "But . . . what if we get caught? What if we get hurt?"

"Then you get caught. And I find myself new sirens. Replacements. It's happened before. Don't think you girls are the only siren candidates in town. Now, I'll hear no more about this." She shakes her head and holds up her hands. "And don't look at me like that, child. I'm not your mother, for goodness' sake. I'm a sea witch! It isn't my job to protect you."

"Fine." I fold my arms across my chest and look at her through my hair. "Ew."

"Lolly." She looks at me, and her expression softens. "I know it's all a bit confusing right now, but you'll see. Things will settle down soon. You'll grow into your full siren self, and then you'll feel much better."

"I don't want to feel better," I tell her. "I don't want to be a siren."

"Here." The Sea Witch gets to her feet and starts rifling through drawers and shelves. "I want you to have something. Close your eyes."

She returns to the table and presses a small, smooth object into my hand. I open my eyes. One side is a small mirror and the other side is an intricate carving of a ship with a giant sea monster clinging to its belly. "This is scrimshaw," she tells me. "It was carved from whale ivory in the eighteenth century. Consider it a birthday gift."

"Why are you giving it to me?"

"Because I want you to see yourself the way I do. Strong. Powerful. You shouldn't be so afraid all the time. Besides, those commercial fishing boats are a menace. The entire shipping industry is, really. It's a brutal, violent, destructive line of work, and it's always been that way. The captain of a ship goes out to conquer and steal. He tears apart the ocean floor. Spills oil in the harbor. I'm ashamed to admit my own family committed some terrible atrocities in the name of industry and the glory of the high seas. That's why I ran away in the first place, you know. That's why I left Barbados when I was still just a child and came to this wretched gray land. I couldn't live with the guilt."

I look up at her, thinking about what Ms. Cross told me.

"Anyway," she continues, "I could tell you of a time when the waters of Maine were teeming with fresh, healthy fish. You couldn't skim a rock off the water without hitting one. Now the local fishermen cut their nets open and it's nothing but stingrays and tin cans. Wrecking those wretched things—it's something to be proud of, really."

"But sometimes you hurt other people too. Local fishermen and sailors who aren't tearing apart the ocean floor."

"Well, yes." She wraps her shawl tighter around her shoulders, and a series of thin silver bracelets clang together on her wrists. "As I told you last night, this sort of magic is . . . It's difficult to control."

I hold up the mirrored side and look at my reflection. "I didn't know you were from Barbados."

"Yes," she says. "From a mansion overlooking the Caribbean Sea. From palm trees and warm wind. From a landscape I will never forget, and like nothing you have anywhere near these dark, bitter waters."

"Why don't you go back, then?"

She sets her cup down on the table and curls her fingers around it. "Our way of life was . . . It was unsustainable. My family did horrible things to make money, to have the life they did. As soon as I was old enough to understand, I knew I wanted no part of it. I left to escape the terrible shame of what they were doing. Little did I know what sort of people I was to encounter here."

She takes another sip of tea. "Suffice it to say that this is not a town that takes kindly to outsiders. It never was."

"Do you . . . do you have a name?"

"Not that you need to concern yourself with, dear."

Her freckled hands around the teacup look as

old and gnarled as driftwood. Centuries older than the rest of her, as if they've lived a different life. They're shaking a little and covered in scars, and I notice for the first time that three of her fingertips are bent at right angles like tiny arrow-heads, broken bones that never healed.

"What happened to you?"

"I believe I'd like to be alone now." She lets go of the cup and blows out the candle. "Run along, please. And tell your dear sisters that the next time they try to change the terms of our agreement, I will chop off their pretty fingers and wear them around my throat. Do you understand?" Her hands go to her neck, and the wolf pads over to the open window and howls at the sky.

I nod and hurry to the door.

Chapter 4

Upon hearing him, the sirens threw themselves
into the sea . . . for they were fated to die when-
ever a man did not fall under their spell.

—*Jorge Luis Borges*

That night, my last night as a half-human
girl, she calls for us again. The humid air
hums with electricity, and we climb from
our beds and head for the beach, raincoats and
boots thrown hastily over our pajamas. It's just like
the journal says we will. We have no choice.

A crescent moon peeks out from behind the
clouds, and we pick our way cautiously among the
rocks, holding hands and weaving, skidding on
pebbles. In the distance lies the ship we are meant
to destroy. As usual, it's some kind of commercial

fishing boat, but a small one, and the wheelhouse is decorated in twinkling white lights.

My sisters begin their song, and I attempt to sing along with them, my voice still broken and unnatural, but improving. Their song is as lovely and alluring as ever, but somehow, the boat continues on its path.

My sisters sing louder, straining, reaching toward the water. They take deep breaths and scream the melody. They stand on the balls of their feet.

The boat passes calmly beneath us.

"Come on!" Lara waves. "Let's get closer."

She leads us down the hillside to the shore. We are slipping in mud, holding on to each other, and I glance over my shoulder, certain something is especially wrong about tonight. Something is different.

We reach the ocean, and they splash right in with all of their clothes still on. Waves lap at their legs and then their waists, and their nightgowns billow around them like jellyfish.

I stay on the sand.

The trawler draws near, slicing like a shark fin

across the wavering reflection of moonlight on the water.

This time is different.

Someone on the ship is playing his own music, a violin concerto in a minor key with double-stops so forceful and strange, you can feel them in your bones. He's playing into a speaker too, so the haunting sound is amplified across the sea.

My sisters are still singing their desperate song, wading deeper and deeper until the water reaches their shoulders.

"Wait!" I start waving my arms and screaming. "Lara! Lula! Lily!"

But this time they are the blind ones. In this state, they can't understand the danger they are in. They can't imagine not getting their way.

There is a creaking, groaning sound, the sound of chains unfurling on a massive spool, and a net is lowered. Normally, these nets trawl the seabed, dredging thousands of pounds of cod, flounder, and haddock from the ocean. But this net is not going to catch anything like that. This net is going to catch my sisters.

From the shore, I scream their names, but I

can only watch as the net hauls all three of them, clinging to each other, from the waves.

I chase the boat all the way back down the shoreline, back to the marina, and I hide behind a stack of lobster traps. The boat docks slowly, and Mr. Bergstrom emerges, making his way down the wooden gangplank. He is carrying Lara, and she is unconscious, her bare arms dangling ghostly white in the moonlight. Two other fishermen follow behind, each holding another of my sisters, also unconscious. While I watch, they take them to the old storage shed at the end of the dock, and then they all disappear inside.

I pull off my rain boots so I won't fall again, and run as fast as I can, barefoot, down the street.

I barely know where I'm going, but somehow I wind up at Jason's house, watching my own ghostly reflection in one of the wall-size windows. The entire place is alarmed, but I know which room is his. I take a handful of broken shells from the walk and toss them at his window. Jason has nightmares, and he never sleeps very deeply. Sure enough, moments later he appears. He glances back over his shoulder and holds up one finger to

let me know he'll be right down. Then he disappears from view. I study myself in the window. I
look like a mess. I'm still carrying my boots, and
my freakish two-tone hair hangs in wet, stringy
waves down my back. All of my clothing—the
nightgown, the moth-eaten wool sweater—is soaking wet and smells like a musty old closet.

Jason re-emerges wearing slippers and a navy
sweatshirt with matching plaid pajama pants. Even
when he's sleeping, he likes his clothes coordinated. "Why are you all wet, Lolly? What happened to your hair?"

"Is your stepdad home?"

He shakes his head. "No, he went with his
buddies on a fishing trip. Are you okay? What's
going on?"

"Just come here!" I motion for him to follow
me behind the enormous oak tree in their side
yard.

"You know I'm mad at you, right?" he says,
crunching behind me through the piles of unraked
leaves. The air smells like pine trees and smoke
from their neighbor's wood-burning stove.

"No, I don't know that. Why?" We stop in

the shadows under the tree, by the crumbling stone wall.

"Because you ran away," he says. "You ran away from me at the dance. Why did you do that?"

"Jason, sit down. There's something I have to tell you."

He leans against the wall and folds his arms across his chest. It's clear out now, and the moon is burning over the ocean like a strange bright scar. It feels as if the temperature is dropping every second, but maybe it's just me, radiating the cold.

Jason's looking at me, and his breath is leaving little puffs of smoke in the air. "Okay. Tell me."

"It's going to sound a bit crazy."

"Just tell me, Lolly! What's going on?"

"You know the old stories about how there are sirens in the harbor?"

"Like, the creatures that lure ships onto rocks?"

"Yes. Like, the monsters."

"Of course. Everyone knows those stories. Sailors used them to explain these eerie cries they'd hear at night and why there were so many shipwrecks around here. It wasn't really monsters

singing, though. It was just the wind through the
caves. It's been proven."

"Well, not exactly."

"What do you mean?"

"I mean, I know for sure that the stories are
true. There are sirens in Starbridge Cove. There
always were."

He looks at me. "How do you know?"

"Because my sisters and I . . . we're living
under this spell. My sisters are already sirens, and
it's going to happen to me too, tomorrow, when
the sun rises on my thirteenth birthday. I don't
want it to happen, but I can't find a way to stop it."

At first he doesn't say anything at all, and I
think, *This is it. This is the actual end of our friendship.* Next
year he'll go off to his fancy prep school and turn
as mean and dull as his stepbrothers. He'll start
sailing and hunting and wearing camouflage base-
ball caps, and he'll forget all about me.

But then he steps away from the wall and grabs
both my hands. "This is incredible."

"Incredible?" My feet slip a little in the grass.
"Jason, you're scared of mayonnaise. You don't
think this is weird?"

"No," he says, and he's still standing there, staring at me like I'm some kind of spirit bear or the biggest giant squid in the universe. "I think it's magical. Lolly, this could change everything."

"But we're in trouble!" I pull my hands out of his grasp and put them on his shoulders so he'll have to pay attention. "There's more I need to explain. You don't understand the whole thing yet."

Wind howls through the branches of the oak tree, knocking them together, and Jason shivers and pulls his fingers into his sleeves. "What else is there to understand? What kind of trouble?"

"It's your stepdad. He's been trapping sirens for years—kidnapping them. He has my sisters now, and maybe some other girls too. I think he's keeping them in the storage shed at the marina."

"Well, we have to do something!" Jason starts looking around the empty yard, like maybe there's someone there who can help us. But of course, there's not. We're all alone out here. "What do we do? Should we call the police?"

"Your stepdad says he basically owns the police. And besides, it's too late for that. When you're a monster, the police can't help you."

Jason kicks at the leaves and his slipper flies off. "I hate him."

"I know."

"You don't, though. You don't know what it's been like living here—the way he treats us."

I look back over my shoulder at the house with its glimmering white walls and darkened windows. "I've seen how he can get."

"He treats my mom like she's just another possession of his, like he owns her. Some nights it gets so bad that she leaves. She goes and sits alone on the beach and cries. I only know because I follow her sometimes."

"Why didn't you tell me?"

"Because I'm going to take care of it. As soon as I turn fifteen, I'm going to get a job on a fishing boat. That's why learning to sail is so important. I have to get used to being out on the water. I have to get us out of here and make my own money so we never have to rely on some creepy guy like him again. So he'll be out of our lives for good."

I reach out and push his hair back from his face, and he gives me a look like maybe that was a weird thing to do.

"You need a haircut," I tell him.

"I know," he says. "I need new shoes, too. He owns four hotels and the entire marina and he makes us walk around with holes in our shoes." Jason shakes his head like he's clearing away some bad memory and puts his arm around my shoulder. "It's okay, Lolly. We'll save your sisters. We'll get them back."

"Aren't you scared? I mean, it's okay if you are. I kind of am."

"I'm not scared," he says. "You know, not all sirens are monsters."

I look up at him. "What?"

"I mean, my stepdad has this book of Norse fairy tales that he's always making us read, and there are these creatures called 'havfrue.' They're not monsters in the usual sense of the word."

"Well, what are they, then?"

"They're like guardians—guardians of the ocean, specifically. I watched a whole documentary about it. Maybe you're one of them."

I think about that for a minute. "Maybe. So you're going to help me, then?"

"Of course I am." He bends to retrieve his

slipper and slides his foot back inside. "Lolly, you're my best friend."

Really, it's kind of awful that someone as nice and color-coordinated as Jason has to have a best friend like me. Probably, I should just leave him alone. Stop getting him into trouble all the time. If I was a good friend, that's what I'd do.

But then, it's just like the Sea Witch said: Sirens make terrible friends.

"Go back inside and get your stepdad's keys to the storage shed," I tell him. "I'll wait for you here."

The storage shed is a place we've been a million times before, a ramshackle wooden structure with a corrugated tin roof where local families keep boats and fishing equipment, and where we used to build secret forts and play hide-and-seek. It's always locked at night, but now we have his step-dad's keys. Jason unlocks the door and pulls it open, and we aim our flashlights and beam them around the inside. It smells like salted fish in there, and even the air feels slimy. Rusted hooks and buoys hang from the ceiling, and stacks of lobster traps and a tangled mess of nets are piled in the corner. We can hear a faint squeaking sound and liquid dripping on the concrete floor.

"They're not here anymore," Jason whispers.

I look at the ground for a moment, trying to remember. "Wait!" I go into the shed and kneel down, running my hands over the cold floor in the darkness. My fingers brush against puddles and sand and cobwebs, and I try not to think about what else. "There's a basement. Remember? Lula hid down there once for hide-and-seek and she got stuck—remember? The door was so heavy, she couldn't get it open again."

"Yeah. But where was it?"

Finally, my fingers brush against a steel ring. "Here!" I grab hold and pull, but the door won't budge. Jason rushes over to help, and we pull together until the door finally starts to lift. "It's heavy! Be careful."

Jason goes around to the other side to push, while I keep pulling at the ring, and we finally get the trapdoor all the way open and propped against the wall.

I look at him. "Ready?"

He nods. "I'll go first."

The steps are steep, nearly vertical, and we have to turn off our flashlights so we can grip the railing with both hands. We lower ourselves into the dank cellar and Jason feels around the walls for a light switch. At last, a dim bulb flickers on above our heads. We hear a faint squeaking sound and the scampering of tiny rodent feet. The nets are still there, wet and tangled, and Lara's locket is lying on the floor, but there is nobody else in the basement. I grab the necklace and slip it on. "What if we can't find them?"

"Come on!" Jason starts climbing back up the ladder. "I have an idea where he might have taken them."

By the time we arrive at our next destination, we're both exhausted and very cold. A red neon sign reads: ARGONAUT MOTEL AND CONDOMINIUMS, and below that: NO VACANCY.

"My stepdad owns this place."

"I know. I remember when they started working on the renovations last year."

"He comes here sometimes when he and my mom are fighting."

The motel is only two stories tall, arranged in a half-moon shape around the parking lot. On the second floor, a plastic tarp starts blowing in the breeze. The rooms up there are still under construction, and they have balconies and sliding glass doors, some of which have been left slightly open. Jason motions for me to follow him and keep quiet.

The main office is small and lit with too-bright fluorescent lights. There are vending machines, a bench, and a fake plant in a wicker pot, and there's a girl wearing a Crew sweatshirt and sleeping with her head on the desk. Behind the desk there is a Peg-Board with room keys hanging on hooks, but we'd never get one without waking her.

Jason shakes his head, and we walk back around to the side of the building, flattening ourselves against the wall to stay out of the path of the flood-lights. There's an abandoned shopping cart filled with blankets, and a jumble of paint cans and buckets in a wire cage.

"It's scary here," I tell him.

"No kidding," he says. "That staircase leads up to the second floor, but I bet all the doors are locked."

"We need to use one of the balcony windows in the back."

"But how are we supposed to reach them?"

"I'll climb up the drainpipe." I take my boots off again and hand them to him. "Meet me at the door."

Jason looks back and forth between me and the rooms, but I'm already gripping the drainpipe and bracing one foot on the bracket that bolts it to the corner of the building. The scales on my feet, it turns out, do make climbing much easier, but my fingernails break, and moths and mosquitoes flutter in my face, and I have to climb toward the floodlights with my eyes closed, trying not to inhale any insects.

I climb until I'm above the balcony and then swing myself over onto the concrete ledge. Then I jump down and peek in through the sliding glass door. And then I turn back and motion for Jason to hurry and come upstairs.

There are strong scents of bleach and paint fumes in the room. The ceiling isn't finished yet and the carpeting hasn't been put down, but the place is crammed with extra furniture: beds, and desks, and stacks of chairs, and hollow glass lamps filled with sand and shells. The only light comes from a ring of tiny candles, flames shivering and casting shadows on the wall. My sisters are lying there in the darkness on one of the beds, still soaking wet and fast asleep. And they're not the only ones. There are other girls asleep in that room, girls with strange hair and scales on their feet. Girls who look a lot like us.

I run to Lara and press my face against her chest. She's breathing, but she won't wake up. None of them will. We call their names, and we poke and pull on their arms, but it's no use. Jason touches Lula's foot, running his finger over her scales. I think it's partly to wake her and partly because he can't believe any of this is real. In any case, she doesn't move. It's like they're all under a spell, a different type of spell.

I look at Jason. He's just standing there blinking, staring at Lula's bare feet. I grab his arm. "We have to get them out of here!"

"I don't think we should move them, Lolly. There's something wrong with them. Like, really wrong. We should call a doctor."

"We're monsters," I whisper. "We don't call the police, and we don't go to the doctor."

"Who takes care of you, then?" he asks. "I mean, when you're sick?"

By the time we reach the Sea Witch's lair, the sun is starting to rise. I haven't slept all night, and I should be even more exhausted, but instead, as we pilot my kayak through the choppy waters, I just feel dizzy and strange. My hands around the paddle are bloody and mosquito bitten, all the nails broken from my climb. The sky is a cold gray color, streaked with pink, and seagulls are starting to call and circle overhead.

We come ashore and drag the kayak to a safe resting place beneath some trees. Jason stares up at the house, and I know he must feel afraid. After all, he's seeing it all for the first time: the weathered gray shingles, the sunken front porch, and the wind chimes made from bird feathers and bones twirling in the breeze.

As usual, the Sea Witch pretends not to know who it is, and she makes a big show of asking before she'll open the door. "Hello? Who's there?" When she does finally open the door, she fusses over Jason. "What an interesting boy. There's something special about him, isn't there?" She touches Jason's hair, and he seems too shocked, or too scared, to do anything about it. "Oh yes. Why, he's a born marauder. A subjugator of the high seas. You have the sea in your veins, don't you, child?" She says it like it's a compliment, but I know how she feels about sailors. It's a defensive maneuver. A trap. If we didn't have a good reason for being there, she'd probably keep on complimenting him and playing with his hair until she lured him right into her kitchen and boiled him in a stew.

"Jason doesn't like the water," I tell her. "He gets seasick."

The Sea Witch snorts and steps aside to let us pass into the kitchen. "You look sickly, Lolly. What's happened? Let me get you both some tea." She walks over to the stove and pours more water in the kettle. "Is Earl Grey all right, young man? Do you take sugar?"

Jason clears his throat. "We don't have time for tea."

She turns to face him. "What?"

"Lolly's sisters are very sick, and we have to rescue them."

"Nonsense," she says, and hands us each a cup. "There's always time for tea. Drink!"

It's nearly impossible to refuse the hospitality of a sea witch, and so Jason and I sit at her table and I take a few sips of the bitter tea. Jason holds his up to his mouth, but I know he's just pretending.

The Sea Witch remains standing, hovering over us. Somewhere, the wolf is growling, a low, guttural sound, like the creaking of a ship.

"So what is it now, Lolly? What's happened to your sisters? And why have you brought this little . . . marauder?"

"My sisters were captured tonight by men on a boat, the ones I told you about. Jason's stepfather was one of them."

She frowns. "Where are they now?"

"We found them at his motel. But there was something wrong with them. They were fast asleep and nothing would wake them. Did you have something to do with this?"

She puts her hands on her hips. "Lolly, why would I do this? Your sisters are my darlings, my soldiers."

"You told me they were replaceable."

"Well, they are. But think practically, dear. They may be replaceable, but who has the time to train a whole new group of girls? Besides, I rather like them. I like all of you. I dare say I've grown quite attached to you these last few months."

Jason puts down his cup and crosses his arms. "Well, who is it, then? Who gave my stepfather the spell? Who taught him how to do something like that?"

The Sea Witch takes a seat at the table. "Sailors have their own ways. When a sea witch drafts sirens into her service, she becomes much more powerful. But it isn't long before sailors learn to fight back, to use their own tricks and magic spells. It becomes a bit of an arms race, you see. Now, this sounds like a classic Norse Sleeping Beauty Spell to me. They were asleep, you said?"

"Yes." Jason leans back in his seat. He keeps glancing over his shoulder at the door, like he may decide to leave at any moment and he wants her to know it.

"And there were candles in a ring?"

"Yes."

"Yes, it's all too familiar. To cast this particular spell, a sailor with the right magical charms need only repeat a protection prayer and then capture the siren in a net of his own making."

"A protection prayer?"

She closes her eyes. *"Odin, far-wanderer, grant me wisdom, courage, and victory. Friend Thor, grant me your strength. And both be with me."* She opens her eyes again and looks at us. "Something to that effect. I've lost many girls to these sorts of spells over the years. In fact, I wouldn't be surprised if your sisters weren't the only ones he's keeping at that motel."

"They're not. We saw other girls asleep in there too."

"Well, unfortunately, there's not much I can do about this. You'll have to go after the person who cast the spell, I'm afraid. That's always the way."

I put my head down on the table. "How?"

"You find his symbol, and you assume its

power. Then you can undo the spell yourself."

"What's a symbol?" Jason asks.

"What's a symbol? Why, a symbol is a represen-
tation, a distillation of the essential, a translation
of the abstract into the concrete. Since the dawn
of time, people have used symbols to make sense of
the universe and its complexities. They carry tremendous power. In fact, one cannot ever dispose
of a symbol. They cannot be thrown away or even
tossed out into the sea. Their power can neither
be created nor destroyed, but only transferred
from one person to another."

I think of my science textbook again, the part
about conservation of energy, where the illustration shows silver spheres on strings that swing back
and forth forever, crashing into each other and
never stopping.

"Transferred to who?" Jason asks.

"To some strong, deserving person for *whom* it
carries equal significance. Might you know anyone
like that, Jason?"

He blushes. "But how . . . how would we do that?"

"You would steal it from him and bury it
someplace important. Someplace meaningful."

She looks up, and her eyes catch the glow from the fire. "Someplace like Fort O'Malley."

"That fort is named for my dad's family," Jason says. "My real dad. General O'Malley was a relative of ours."

"Well." The Sea Witch looks at him with what could maybe be mistaken for kindness. "Imagine that."

"But it's not there anymore. They say it was completely destroyed in the War of 1812."

"Oh, it was destroyed more times than that!" She laughs. "For two hundred years, the army kept building it up, only to see it torn down by invading forces. Why, that fort never met a battle it could withstand. I believe it holds the record for most destroyed fort of all time."

"Oh." Jason slumps down a little in his seat.

"But the roots of the place, the earthworks, were incredibly strong. They withstood all of that violence and destruction for hundreds of years. And what most people don't realize is that the original Fort O'Malley, the foundation, is still there."

"But taking the symbol to the fort . . . why is

that better than just throwing it away, throwing it into the ocean?"

"Because things have a way of returning from the bottom of the sea, don't they? Even the heaviest items sometimes float back to the surface when you least expect them. And this act, burying the symbol in a place that has significance, this will transfer its power to you. Do you think you're ready for something like that?"

Jason sits up straight again and pushes his shoulders back. "Yes," he says. "I've been ready for a long time."

"Well, it won't be easy. In the old days, the Viking kings all had crowns or helmets as symbols of their power. I don't know what kind of symbol your stepfather has."

"He has this crown that he's completely obsessed with. He keeps it locked up all the time and wears the key around his neck. I bet that's his symbol. But how do we find Fort O'Malley?"

"With a map, of course." She heaves herself up from her chair and moves across the room. "I'll show you both." She pulls a giant nautical map from a shelf and spreads it across the kitchen table. "Something tells me you're a man who knows his way around a map. Is it true? Can you read a map like this?"

"Yes," Jason says. "I study maps like this all the time."

She nods. "As you should. Now look, this region is filled with tiny islands. Hundreds of them. Each has its own magic, its unique creatures and geological oddities. Some have waterfalls, and some have exotic animals, strange bears, and parrots, tortoises, and sea serpents—all things escaped from shipwrecks hundreds of years ago. Now, these . . ." She starts tracing one gnarled finger in circles over a place just a few miles north of us. "These are the Ursid Islands, islands riddled with canyons and volcanic craters. According to legend, you'll find the ruins of Fort O'Malley there."

"According to legend? You've never been there yourself?"

"Oh, goodness no. The coastline is far too dangerous up there, shallow and rocky. There's nowhere to properly dock a boat, and I certainly don't fancy a swim. But if you were willing to go, I would gladly assist in any way I could."

"But how do we know we can trust you?" Jason asks. "I mean, Lolly says you're supposed to be some sort of witch, right? And what if that's not even true? What if you're actually just some crazy person?"

She narrows her eyes. "Young man, 'witch' is in the eye of the beholder. It's just a name. A label. For example, I might call you a 'little marauder' just because you are clearly a descendant of the very seafaring people who first colonized this land, treated me like an animal, and banished me to this lonesome existence, and therefore you are my enemy."

"You did call me that."

"Well, there you are. But we also have an enemy in common, which, some would say, makes us allies. So let's not talk of witches and thieves and try to figure out who is or isn't crazy. That's nearly always a waste of time. Names, labels, they mean whatever you want them to mean. And a word that means whatever you want it to mean is actually, well, *meaningless*."

Jason frowns. "I guess you're right."

"Of course I am." The Sea Witch taps the map

with her finger. "Now then, let's focus on the task at hand, shall we?"

"How would we even steal the crown, though?" I ask. "I mean, he never lets that key out of his sight."

The Sea Witch dismisses the idea with a wave of her hand. "I can give you a potion that will render your stepfather temporarily unconscious, knock him out long enough for you to steal his crown. How does that sound?"

Jason looks totally on board now. "I think that sounds great!"

She walks across the room to a massive wardrobe that stands beside the fireplace. She unlocks the cupboard, and the doors creak on their hinges and sweep apart, revealing shelves filled with tiny jars. Each of the jars contains a potion that bubbles or shimmers or changes color in the light. She chooses one and holds it up, and a thick, sparkling liquid swirls inside. "You must be careful with it, of course," she warns us. "A few drops are powerful enough to rob a grown man of all his strength. Dissolve it in a person's drink, and he will be inca-pacitated for hours."

"That's exactly what we need." Jason gets up and tries to grab the potion, and the Sea Witch holds the jar above her head.

"Young man," she says. "A sea witch will neither suffer fools nor tolerate rudeness."

"I'm sorry." He looks at the floor. "May I have the potion, please?"

"Yes you may."

She hands it to him, and he slips it in his pocket.

"But giving my stepfather this potion, robbing him of his strength, that won't be enough to break the spell?"

"Correct," she tells us. "Now, this point is important, so listen closely, all right? It is not enough to hurt him. To wound him. To kill him, even. That does nothing for you. You have to assume his power yourself, and then you have to be the one to undo the spell. Like this."

She reaches across the table and traces a crescent shape on my forehead with her finger. "Smear one of them with the dirt from the place where you bury the crown, and then say these words." She says some words in a language I can't understand. "You see?"

Jason seems a little uncertain. "I have to do that to her sisters?"

"You can do it to Lolly, if you prefer. She'll be a siren then too. Perform that spell on any one of them, you see, and you wake up all the others. Think you've got it?"

Jason repeats the spell back perfectly, and the Sea Witch takes a seat. "Well done," she says. "You learn quickly."

"He's in honors Spanish," I tell her.

Then she leans sideways and whispers in his ear. "You have quite the interesting friendship here, you know. A boy with the sea in his blood and the newest siren in Starbridge Cove. Aren't you just the tiniest bit worried? Afraid she'll break your heart? Or worse?"

Jason pushes her away. "Why don't you just let them all go?"

For a moment, the Sea Witch appears paralyzed. "You mean, return them to their former human state?"

"Yes. That's exactly what I mean. Why are you doing this to them?"

She tosses her shawl over her shoulders and the

mocking smile disappears from her face. "Young man, this is not a thing that I am doing to them. This is a thing that they asked me for. In fact, if I told you what I know about the night their mother died, you would not be so quick to judge me or speak to me in this tone."

"What are you talking about?"

She folds her arms prettily on the table and looks at me. "I am not at liberty to say."

I lean forward in my chair, as desperate to hear what she knows as the sailors are to hear whatever it is they hear when we sing to them. "If you know something about my mom," I tell her, "about that night, I want to know it too. Please."

The Sea Witch reaches for the teapot, and the angles of her collarbone protrude. "Your mother . . . she was not alone out there on the bridge that night like everybody thinks she was."

"What do you mean?"

She pours more tea in my cup. "I mean you were out there too. Do you understand? You were with her in the car."

"But I don't—"

"No, you wouldn't remember, dear. But that's

the real reason your sisters made this bargain. They'd lost you, you see. You drowned in the river along with your mother. And so they came to me in the dead of night, pale and hollowed out with grief, and they sat right here at my table, right where you are now, and they told me they were desperate to have you back. I told them they could make a trade: their souls for their sister. And they agreed. That's always what this was about, Lorelei. This was a sacrifice they made."

Jason gets up from the table. "No," he says. "No! Don't believe her, Lolly. She's just trying to hurt you." He turns to the Sea Witch. "Why would you tell her something like that? You're horrible."

"Horrible?" Red blotches appear on her neck, beneath her freckled skin. "Who are you to call me horrible? I'm the one who saved her. What have you ever done?"

"I think you're a liar," he says. "I think you're just using them, and now they're hurt, and I think this whole thing is your fault!"

"You know nothing!" The Sea Witch sweeps the teapot from the table and it falls to the ground and shatters.

Out of the darkness comes a click-clicking of claws on the wooden floor, and then the wolf is in the room with us, wild and monstrous with his matted fur and sharp yellow eyes, and ribbons of drool hang from his mouth.

Jason's face turns pale. "What—what is that?"

"Oh," I tell him. "That's her wolf. He just—"

But then the wolf starts barking like crazy, and he raises himself up on his hind legs and lunges at Jason.

"Stop it!" The Sea Witch gets up and yanks the wolf backward. He loses his balance and skids on the floor. "No more of this!" She gives him a shove, and he whimpers and pads away down the hall.

"He clawed me," Jason says. Jason, whose shirt is now stained with blood and whose stricken face is white and slicked with sweat.

"Oh dear." The Sea Witch looks at me. "The wound is deep."

This is an understatement. In fact, it's a good thing Jason can't see what's happening because it's completely horrifying.

"Do something!" I tell her. "He's hurt!"

"All right, now. Just a second. Let's not get hysterical here." She leads Jason back to the cabinet of potions, sits him on a stool, and pulls down a glass jar, a needle, and a spool of blue thread. She puts the jar up to his mouth and pours some liquid down his throat. Then she licks the thread and slips it through the needle, and she starts sewing up the gash on his shoulder as if his skin were torn pieces of fabric.

"Oh, don't look so frightened," she says, glancing at me. "These medicines are very powerful, and this is a special, healing thread. He'll be fixed up in no time. You know, by the time I was your age, I was bribing my way onto a whaling ship bound for the New World. You children are different now, I suppose. Softer." She breaks the thread with her teeth and ties a knot. Then she kneels to Jason's eye level. "I am sorry, young man. I don't let people in my home very often. I don't trust people easily."

Jason touches his shoulder with the tips of his fingers, and when he speaks his voice is a whisper. "I don't either."

The Sea Witch lifts her chin in the direction of the living room, which is a small room set farther back in the house—a room she's never invited us to

before. "Let's go sit by the fire and collect ourselves, shall we? I believe this has been rather a
trying encounter for us all."

The wolf is already there, curled beneath the
window, and we hesitate to get near him again, but
she pushes us forward. "Go on," she says. "He
won't hurt you now. I swear."

Jason and I sit on the rug, and the Sea Witch
takes off her shawl and wraps it around us both
like a blanket. Beneath my skin, my bones feel like
icicles, and there is a strange humming sound in
my head. The fire pops and sparks, and it's so
warm, I wish I could crawl right inside.

She sits in a rocking chair and pats the wolf on
his head. "I apologize again on his behalf," she
tells us. "He is very protective of me."

Jason nods. "I'm sorry I said you were horrible."

"Well, you're certainly not the first."

I inch closer to the fire, and the humming gets
louder. "I want to know more about the night of
the accident."

She starts rocking the chair with the balls of her
feet and narrows her eyes. "Such as?"

"Such as, well, where were we going?"

"According to your sisters, your mother was driving you home from some sort of gymnastics competition. As you know, we had a terrible winter last year; the roads were covered in ice. Apparently, your father told her to stay the night, but she insisted on driving back home."

I search my memory for some image or sensation from that night. Glistening roads, hail pinging off the roof of the car, icicles hanging from the bridge. My mother stops singing with the radio for a moment, glances at me in the warm semidarkness of the car, and tries to smile. I'm holding a box of chicken nuggets in my lap, and I can tell that something is wrong. Something bad's about to happen. But I don't know if those memories are real or made up or from some other night entirely.

"So it was my fault, then, what they did. It was because of me." I'm sure I'm speaking out loud, but the humming in my head has become a roar, like the ocean, and my voice sounds so distant, like it's being filtered through a speaker and broadcast from a million miles away.

"But—" Jason looks up. "If Lolly was in that car, if she had—if something had happened to her, we all would have heard about it, right? Wouldn't we remember?"

The Sea Witch shakes her head. "That was part of the bargain, you see. They were to go out to the graveyard and exhume her body, carry her home, and tuck her in her bed, and in the morning she'd be awake again, their little sister, good as new, as if she'd never left. And nobody in town, including her, would have any memory of what happened that night. Those sorts of community spells, the erasing of unpleasant memories from a large group of like-minded people, are among the easiest to perform. Much simpler than raising the dead." She smooths my hair back. "You see, your sisters don't really love being sirens. Or maybe they do. I suppose I couldn't say. But what motivated them originally, the reason they came to me and made this trade in the first place, was to save you."

The wolf whimpers in his sleep, and she scratches behind his ears. "Now, these sorts of transformations take a toll on the body. Quite soon, dear, you're going to be in excruciating agony. Once that happens, if I try to change you back, it could cost you your life. And so that, young man, is why I wouldn't dream of it."

"But if you can do this, if you can bring people back from the dead, why didn't you bring their mother back too?"

"Oh, a trip to the underworld is an exhausting journey. Picture a bus ride in traffic on a rainy afternoon. Or the helpless desperation of the wait for a stalled baggage carousel at the airport."

"I've never been to the airport," Jason tells her.

"Take my word for it then, dear. It is most unpleasant. Besides, magic like this won't work for everyone. I can only bring certain girls back. Outsiders. Motherless girls with a predilection for music. Girls whom I can then use as sirens to lure ships to our shore."

"Why do they have to be girls?"

"I don't make the rules, Jason. I didn't invent this system. I merely figured out a way to operate within it."

I remember a dream I once had of a hallway, like a bright hospital corridor. The smell of salt-water. The burn of blood returning to my veins.

I can feel it now.

I try to stand, but my legs won't hold. It's as if my bones have melted right out from inside me. "There's something wrong with me."

"No, there's nothing wrong." The Sea Witch takes a watch out of the pocket of her dress and smiles. "Everything is exactly right."

"What's happening?" Jason asks.

"She's becoming a siren. The transformation is complete."

"Now?"

"Yes, Lolly is thirteen years old today. Surely *you* know that. Wish her a happy birthday."

It hits me before I can do or say anything else. There is a feeling like a lead weight falling through my stomach, and then the whole room seems to tilt. Jason lets me lean on him, and we stumble back into the kitchen, and I feel too sick to even care how disgusting I must look.

The Sea Witch follows us. "Take her outside," she advises. She kneels and begins gathering the pieces of her broken teapot. "Things are bound to get a bit messy now."

Chapter

5

Sirens appeal to the spirit, not to the flesh.
—*Jane Ellen Harrison*

When I wake up, the first thing that happens is I roll onto my side and throw up all over the sand. I pull off my boots to check my feet and ankles, and they're completely covered in scales now, bright, thick, bottle-green scales. My hair is nearly white.

I get up and stagger to the edge of the shore, and I start yelling at the ocean. I know it's crazy, but I can't stop. "I hate you!" I start screaming, and throwing rocks into the waves, as if I could hurt them. As if my fury could change anything. "I hate you!"

When I'm too cold and tired to yell at the ocean anymore, I sit back on the sand. I pick up one last pebble and hurl it away down the beach.

Jason waits a few minutes before coming to sit with me. Normally, I would die of embarrassment that he witnessed that whole display, but right now I don't even care. I'm sure he's terrified. I'm shocked he's even still here.

"It's like I told you before," he says. "You're not a monster. You're a guardian."

I sniff, and look at him through my hair. "It's the same thing."

He reaches out and wraps his fingers around my ankle.

"What are you doing?"

"I want to see your scales."

"No! Stop. It's gross. You don't want to see."

"Wait a second." He touches my foot.

"I said stop!" I move a few feet away from him and sit down again with my arms wrapped around my legs and my head down. "I can't believe you did that."

"Lolly, I was just kidding around. I'm sorry."

I look down at my bare feet. A week ago, Lula painted my toenails bright green to match the scales. It seemed cool at the time, but now it looks totally ridiculous. I try to curl my toes into the sand. "Just stop talking, please."

"Listen, I don't . . . I don't think it's gross. Really." Jason walks over and sits next to me. "You know, if you could just stop causing shipwrecks, you'd be fine. You wouldn't hurt anybody and nobody would want to hurt you."

"But I don't think I can. I mean, you heard her. I can't control it. *She* can't even control it really. I'm a monster—a mystery of the deep. I might as well be a giant squid."

"Well, I love giant squids. They can withstand an enormous amount of pressure, you know. They can survive in some of the most hostile environments on the planet."

"Okay, you *admire* giant squids. But you wouldn't want to be best friends with one."

"Who knows?" Jason reaches up and touches the scar on his shoulder. His shirt is all torn and spattered with blood, but that doesn't seem to bother him now.

"It's already fading," I tell him. "Don't worry. You can barely see it."

"I don't care about that." He gets to his feet
and grabs a nearby stick. "Come on! We have to
stop my stepfather and save your sisters. That's all
that matters."

"But I'm a siren now," I tell him. "Like, officially."

"I know. So what?"

This strange tiredness is settling over my body.
A heaviness. I don't think I could do a cartwheel
now if my life depended on it. I think about my
sisters and how, since they became sirens, they
don't really play outside or run around or anything. I used to get mad at them for it. "Jason, I
don't know if sirens do this sort of thing."

"What sort of thing?"

"Well, what if she's lying about the symbol?
What if she's lying about everything? What if she
just wants to hurt us?"

Jason breaks the stick in half and hands me a
piece. "We have a common enemy. She was right
about that. Now, I know what we can do. The festival starts in six hours, and he'll have the crown
with him there. We can steal it during the parade
and bring it to the fort first thing the next morning. I'll sail us there myself."

"But we're still wearing pajamas. And you're covered in blood."

"We'll stop at my house and change."

"But what if your stepdad's there?"

"He told us he'd be away all night before the festival, putting the finishing touches on his knarr. Come on!" He takes his end of the stick and taps it against mine. "This is our chance. Finally. And who cares if you're a siren? You can still decide what you want to do."

"I think that's easy for you to say." I hold up my part of the stick, which is pronged like a wishbone, and look at him through the forked end. "What are we doing with these?"

"We're not doing anything with them. Come on, now you're just being annoying."

"Okay. Fine." I get up slowly from the sand.

"Are you ready?" he asks.

"Ready." I take the stick and point it in the direction of his house. "Let's go."

We get back to Jason's house and scan the premises for signs of his stepdad. His truck is nowhere to be found, and his boots and coat are missing from the front hallway, so we determine that the coast is clear. Then Jason sneaks up to his room to change while I wait in the kitchen and try to think of a lie about why I'm there. A flyer for the festival is sitting on the counter, and because I don't know what else to do with myself, I pick it up and start reading through the schedule of events.

THE ANNUAL SALT AND STARS FOLK FESTIVAL

SPONSORED BY BISHOP'S FISH AND VIKING INDUSTRIES

DAY ONE

4 P.M.: GRAND HIGH PARADE

AND SUNRISE COUNTY PUBLIC SCHOOL ASSEMBLY

6 P.M.: SUNSET CONCERT

DAY TWO

9 A.M.: PANCAKE BREAKFAST

(HOSTED BY THE STARBRIDGE DINER)

6 P.M.: FIREWORKS DISPLAY

"Lolly, honey?" Alice enters the kitchen wearing slippers and a pink silk bathrobe. Without makeup on, she looks like a faded watercolor version of herself. "What are you doing here, sweetheart?"

"Oh, Jason and I are going to walk to school together this morning. We have an early dress rehearsal."

"You let your sisters do that to your hair?" She bustles around the kitchen, tossing a few slices of bread into the toaster and flipping the switch on the coffeepot.

I tap my fingers on the counter. "Um, yes."

She shakes her head. "You girls. I remember when Lily tried to give Jason a haircut. Do you remember that? He was practically bald."

"I remember," I tell her.

"You know, you look a little . . . tired. Are you feeling okay? Can I get you anything?"

"I'll take some coffee."

She raises one eyebrow. "Aren't you a little young for coffee?" But she puts a napkin and a mug in the shape of a moose head down on the counter in front of me. "I guess you kids start everything early these days."

"I guess so."

"Do you take milk?"

"I'll just drink it black."

As soon as we walk through the front doors of the school, Coach Bouchard grabs us and pushes us toward the gym, where about eighty middle and elementary school students dressed as indigenous fish, foliage, and animals are warming up on wind instruments and practicing dance routines. A second-grade girl wearing a giant jellyfish hat with streamers is standing in the middle of the room sobbing, and a school of third-grade goldfish is trying to console her. Meanwhile, an eighth-grade moose narrowly misses stabbing me with her antlers. "Move, seventh grader!"

"Attention, people!" In deference to his authority as official festival choreographer, the school has outfitted Coach Bouchard with a new megaphone. "Attention!"

We cover our ears against the squeal of feedback.

"Find your costumes!"

I trudge to the pile marked 7TH-GRADE SHELL-FISH and start sifting through antennae, while Jason looks for the sign saying 8TH-GRADE FOLIAGE.

I grab my costume, and then I look up and notice Emma flipping through a rack of mermaid tails, which are actually just long, sparkly skirts so the mermaids can still perform their gymnastics routines. "Oh," she says. "It's you."

"Yeah," I tell her. "It's me."

"You look awful. What's wrong with your hair?"

"What do you mean?"

"Did you bleach it? That's really bad for you, you know. You could lose all your hair that way. I mean, it looks almost white—"

"Emma, we've never really liked each other."

"Well, that's true. What's your point?"

"Okay, um . . . I want to know if I can ask for your help with something."

"With what?"

"Well, as a mermaid, you have special access to the grand high float."

"Of course I do." She tosses her ponytail. "That's only natural."

"Right. And as a snail, I don't have any access at all."

"That's the circle of life, Lolly."

I'm tempted to argue with her, but it's

difficult to debate social justice in the mermaid kingdom when you're wearing antennae. "Okay, so what I'm wondering is if you can pour something into the Viking's goblet. And make sure he drinks it."

She wrinkles her nose. "Why would I do that?"

Jason comes up behind us. "Because he's my stepdad," he says. "And we're playing a trick on him. Like, a prank."

"Oh!" Emma tosses her hair again. Her eyes light up at the mere sight of Jason, and her voice goes up about three octaves. "I love pranks. Is this your idea, *Jay*?"

"Um, yeah."

"That's so cool."

"Okay, so you'll do it?"

"Sure. Give me the drink."

I hand it to her, and she holds it up to her face. "What's in there? It looks like nail polish."

"It's a long story," Jason says. "Just make sure he drinks it."

She salutes him. "Will do! Now, if you'll excuse me." She loops her mermaid tail over one arm. "I have to go to my dressing room."

† † †

At three forty-five, grades one through seven are lined up in the hallway, awaiting our cue. I tried hiding when Nurse Claire came through to do everybody's makeup, but she caught me, so now I'm wearing my full snail regalia: brown stockings, a puffy white tutu, antennae, the giant cardboard shell, green glitter eyeliner, and blue mascara. With moments to go before the big opening number, I climb the radiator and pull myself into a crouching position on the windowsill. Outside, it's a beautiful fall day, clear and cold with the sun just starting to set, but I can't feel anything except worried and a little sick. I can't stop thinking about my sisters frozen in the motel and what we're about to do to Mr. Bergstrom.

And what if it doesn't work?

And what if it does?

At last, I see the parade winding its way up the main road. At Mr. Bergstrom's insistence, each float is lined with flaming torches, and from this distance, the entire thing looks like one long dragon of fire. The Sunrise County Middle School marching band leads the way, and Mr. Bergstrom follows close behind, riding his float shaped like a Viking ship. Middle school mermaids flip and cartwheel around him while he sits atop his throne, wearing his crown and waving his flaming torch in the air. From my lookout, I can see that one rogue pinecone, Jason, has already broken free of the eighth-grade group and is edging closer to the float.

As the parade reaches the main doors of the school, Jason's stepdad hands his torch to one of the mermaids for safekeeping. Then he reaches for his goblet. According to the script, he's supposed to say, "Hand me my drink, for I am ready to carouse!"

Emma hands him his goblet.

I slip my arms out of my shell and stay curled in a ball with my antennae pressed to the glass and my fingers crossed.

Within seconds, Mr. Bergstrom stops shouting his lines and shuts his eyes. And then, just like that, he topples over. He falls off his plywood throne and lands in a heap on the glittery, felt-covered floor, and his crown goes rolling right off his head.

At first, everyone is silent. Stunned. The marching band stops playing, and the dancers stop dancing, and everyone stares in disbelief.

Finally, someone asks, "Is this part of the show?"

And then everything happens at once. Everyone starts rushing around, talking over each other and shouting for help.

"Call an ambulance!"

"Help him!"

"What's happening?"

"Looks like a heart attack!"

"Extinguish the torches!"

In the midst of the commotion, Jason grabs the fallen crown from the edge of the float. "I'm his stepson," he tells the crowd. "I'll keep this safe." People stand aside to let him pass, and then he takes off, running to our meeting place behind the school. An ambulance sounds in the distance, and I hop down from my perch on the windowsill and race into the hallway, shoving crowds of little kids in fish costumes out of my way.

Emma comes bursting in through the front doors and barrels right into me. "What did you do?" she hisses. "Did we just, like, kill him?"

I pull her into the corner. "No," I tell her. "Calm down. It's—"

"Don't tell me it's a long story!"

"It'll be fine," I tell her. "He's not— We didn't kill him. Just don't say anything, okay?"

"What would I say? You think I want to get blamed for this?"

We hear another squeal of feedback and then Coach Bouchard's voice comes over the megaphone. "He's all right, ladies and gentlemen! Everyone remain calm. I'm hearing now that he's conscious and stable and they'll be taking him to Sunrise County General for observation."

"See?"

Emma shakes her head. "You know, you and Jason can have each other. You're both, like, too weird to deal with."

"Fine," I tell her.

"Fine," she says.

Jason and I meet at the old basketball court behind the Dumpsters, where nobody ever goes. The asphalt is uneven and the hoops are threaded with rusty steel chains.

"Are you sure we can't just go to the island now?" I ask him.

"It'll be dark soon, and we won't be able to find the island or Fort O'Malley." Jason is still hugging the crown to his chest. "I'll keep this," he tells me. "And we'll go first thing in the morning, okay? As soon as it's light."

"Okay." I nod. "I'll meet you back at the dock in the morning."

He shifts the crown to his hip. "Don't you think I should go home with you?"

"To my house?"

"Yeah. I mean, just to make sure you're safe there by yourself."

I look at the cracks in the pavement. "No," I tell him. "I mean, I'll be fine." *Also, I'm afraid you might want to kiss me again and I won't know how, and then you'll change your mind about liking me. Or maybe, now that I'm an undead zombie monster, you won't try to kiss me at all and that would be even worse.*

Jason kicks at some loose gravel with his sneaker. "Okay," he says. "Then I guess I'll see you in the morning."

"I'll see you in the morning," I tell him. "Definitely."

We look at each other for a second, and it's like one of those weird moments where you know you're making an important choice. Like you can almost feel yourself as an adult looking back and thinking about that moment and the choice you made. But you don't know yet if it was the right one or the wrong one.

By the time I climb the driveway and put my key in the lock, it's nearly dark. The second I walk in the door, I realize I can't remember the last time I was alone in our house. Everything looks different. There are all kinds of strange shadows lurking everywhere, and the floorboards creak under my feet. The radiators all start hissing at once, and it's pretty much the scariest sound I've ever heard. I can't even bring myself to go upstairs and change out of my snail costume. Instead, I lock the front door and run down to the basement to grab Dad's pistol from its hiding place behind the dryer. Even loaded with blanks, it scares me, and I don't like touching it, but not having it feels worse. I slide it into my schoolbag and hurry back into the living room, where I leap onto the couch and pull a knit afghan up over my shoulders and face so only my eyes are peeking out.

The wind picks up and the weather vane on the roof starts to creak. I remember what Jason's mom said about us. *They're so vulnerable up there in that house.* At the time, I didn't understand what she meant. But now the loneliness is overwhelming. There's nobody to notice if I disappear. I could just vanish into thin air.

I stay awake for a long time, terror crawling like cold spiders down my scalp. For some reason, I keep thinking about this time after my mom died, the first time I went into her room alone and saw her glasses sitting there folded on the night table. I thought, *She's gone, but her glasses are still here.* It was like a terrible arithmetic I couldn't wrap my mind around. Mom's glasses minus Mom equals what?

I think about maybe calling Jason and telling him I was wrong after all, that I should have let him come over. But now it's practically the middle of the night. And what if his mom answers? What if Mr. Bergstrom answers? Instead, I reach into my schoolbag and pull out Hannah's diary and one of Lula's old sweatshirts. I pull the sweatshirt on right over my costume, clasp my arms around my knees, and curl up as tight as I can with the book propped open on the pillow next to me.

June 23rd, 1705

My mind is racked with terrible dreams. It's been nearly six months since the Morgana sailed from Bishop's Harbor, and still no word from Rebecca. She is such a sweet child, innocent of the events that brought her into the world. I sent her away from this village to keep her safe, yet I fear I put her life in danger. Perhaps the Morgana was lost at sea. Perhaps the captain never brought her ashore. Either way, I shall have no rest until I find her again. Neither will any of the sea captains or fishermen in this town. Rebecca is the only good thing I ever had in my life, and her memory, the ghost of her, is always in my thoughts. It may drive me mad. I fear it already has. But if it takes an eternity, I will never stop searching for her. And they will suffer for what they have done. Once, I learned a dark magic to protect myself. Now, again, I shall use it.

† † †

I wake hours later to the sound of car wheels crunching up the driveway. It's still pretty dark out, and I watch as the reflection from a pair of head-lights travels slowly across the ceiling. My first thought, automatically, is: *Mom. She's home,* as if I fell asleep on the couch waiting up for her. But then I come more fully awake and the reality of everything comes crashing back around me. It can't be her; it's somebody else. Afraid all over again, I curl my fingers through the holes in the blanket.

Outside, a car door opens and slams and foot-steps shuffle across the gravel and up the front steps. "Lorelei!"

It's Mr. Bergstrom out there on the porch again, calling me and ringing the bell, tapping on the window. He's wearing his work gloves, and he has a crowbar slung over his shoulder. "I see you in there, young lady. I see you."

He starts digging at the lock with the crowbar, and I grab my schoolbag and slip my arms through the strap just as he bursts into the entryway. He looks like a giant, standing here in our house, backlit beside our collection of framed school photos and Lara's spelling bee certificate. The door is hanging half off its hinges, and there's cold air blowing through the living room, scattering papers across the floor.

"You're not allowed to just come in here!" I try to make my voice sound brave. I point at him the way I once saw Ms. Cross point at some older boys she found smoking behind the school. "This is my house! I live here. You can't just come in."

But Mr. Bergstrom ignores me, waving the crowbar around like a conductor of the world's most violent and ridiculous orchestra, and I realize that yes, he can come in. I'm alone here, and I'm a lot smaller than him, and there's actually nothing I can do to stop him.

Mr. Bergstrom takes his crowbar and starts smashing things. He smashes the lamp on the coffee table, and a framed article about my dad's first album, and the vase my mom used to keep filled with flowers. He smashes a glass cabinet full of my grandparents' dishes and trinkets from their old house. In less than a minute, our entire living room is destroyed. I want to scream, but I'm too scared now. I can't make my voice work.

Mr. Bergstrom drops the crowbar and starts walking toward me. "You're coming with me now." He keeps coming closer, so I have to keep backing up, until I'm pressed flat against the wall with nowhere else to go. His enormous frame is looming in front of me, and I have to crane my neck to see his face. "Get your shoes on," he says.

We drive a while in silence, me sitting in the back behind the passenger seat. Mr. Bergstrom keeps looking at me over his shoulder, and, every time, he nearly swerves off the road.

"I know you're a nice girl," he says. "This isn't about that. But you're still a predator, just like all the others. And me, my sons, my crew, and every other sailor in our harbor, we're all at risk. Am I right?" He meets my eyes in the rearview mirror and smiles like we have a secret together.

"No," I say. "I don't want to hurt anybody."

"Well, that wasn't exactly my question." The smile disappears from his face, and he rolls down the window and spits. "That's the problem with your kind. You twist things, and you lie. You pretend, and you make promises. And then what happens? You hurt and kill us. Destroy our property. Now, when something like this happens, you only have yourself to blame. You and your sisters and all the others just like you."

I look out the window. All the trees are bare, and the dawn sky is as thick and white as cotton. There's nobody else on the road. Everything is empty and quiet, and I watch the highway drift beneath our wheels.

"Do you know where we're going?"

I nod. "To the marina. You're going to trap me in a net and cast a spell on me, just like you did my sisters."

"It doesn't hurt," he explains. "The spell, I mean. You won't feel a thing."

I shift in my seat and clutch the bag closer to my chest. "How do you know?"

The marina finally comes into view, boats bobbing on the water. Some are already strung with red and green Christmas lights. Out on the main road, I see a flash of bright blue through the trees, and I know it's Jason coming to meet me.

I glance at Mr. Bergstrom, but he doesn't

notice. He comes around the car and grabs my arm. "Let's go."

It's much colder on the water. We board one of the fishing boats at the back of the marina, an older vessel streaked with rust and swaying slightly in the waves. The winches, spooled with sinister green nets, are taller than I am. "I'll be right back." Mr. Bergstrom lets go of me, and my feet skid on the slippery surface of the deck. He disappears into the wheelhouse, and I take the pistol out of my bag. It startles me a little, just the coldness and the sight of it out in the world. I'm not even sure what to say to announce its presence. *Surprise?*

I feel the wind pick up, blowing wisps of platinum hair across my face.

"Um, excuse me?" I clear my throat. "Mr. Bergstrom?"

"What?"

"Look. Look at this."

"What now?" Mr. Bergstrom turns. He sees the pistol and lifts his hands in the air. He sort of laughs and sort of snorts. "What do you think you're going to do with that?"

I fire the gun. It kicks back and knocks against my face, and for a few seconds, I can't even see straight. I bring my fingers to my forehead and feel warm, sticky blood in my hair. Mr. Bergstrom is ducking on the deck, and I drop the gun and fumble for the railing, swing my legs over the ladder, and climb until I can feel the dock again beneath my feet.

Chapter 6

And soon they saw a fair island . . . where
the clear-voiced Sirens . . . used to beguile
with their sweet songs whoever cast anchor
there, and then destroy him.
—*The Argonautica*

I find our little green kayak and push it into the
water, trying to balance as small waves lap the
sides. I can get myself to the fort, I think, and
meet Jason there. It's light out now, but there
are storm clouds gathering. In the distance, I
think I hear Mr. Bergstrom start up the motor
on his boat.

Thunder rumbles softly in the distance and
freezing sea spray stings my face as I paddle
unsteadily beyond the safety of the harbor. I have

to sail against the wind, and my arms and stomach muscles ache with the strain of keeping the little boat on course. A storm is coming. And maybe I've made a terrible mistake. Maybe this whole thing is a trap. Maybe the Sea Witch is sending us all to our deaths. Maybe Fort O'Malley really was destroyed in the War of 1812 and there's nothing at the end of this journey but a massive squall and an island that doesn't exist.

But then I see it. It appears like a vision in the water, smaller than I pictured, but just as the Sea Witch described. The shoreline is jagged and dangerous, and the current swirls all around like a million tiny whirlpools. Strange seabirds perch solemnly along the uneven ridge of the cliffs, watching.

A huge wall of water slams the side of the kayak, and the little boat capsizes, dumping me into the freezing waves. I cling to it and kick the rest of the way to the beach, and I drag myself onto the sand and lie there with the tide rising all around, looking up at the trees. Shrouded in mist, they look like long, skinny arms. My head is filled with the sound of my own labored breathing, and my heartbeat, and the rushing of the water from the ocean and the storm.

I roll onto my stomach and look out at the water. Mr. Bergstrom's boat is speeding toward me, and a familiar pulling sensation, bigger than the cold and the pain, starts in my throat. I crawl to the very edge of the beach, to where the ground becomes soggy and waves lap at the shore, and I close my eyes and try to clear my mind.

My sisters always say that being a good siren is mostly listening. People think it's all about the singing, but really it's the other way around. You have to be able to hear people. The singing comes last. Now, I start to hear something like a radio transmission from out at sea. It's just static at first, layered with the sound of many voices all whispering at once, but I concentrate as hard as I can, and at last, I start to hear Mr. Bergstrom's voice separate from the rest. It's not his thoughts I hear; it's more like his wishes, his hopes. They grow and build and flutter around in my mind like moths. The song has to be crafted especially for him. It has to promise him power and violence, because that's what he wants. That's what he desires most of all.

A perfect ribbon of melody emerges from my throat. At last, I sound exactly like my sisters. It feels so natural to me too, like the first time I landed a handspring on the balance beam in gymnastics, that split second after tumbling in space when I felt the beam beneath my feet and knew exactly where I was.

It works.

In spite of the storm and the danger, Mr. Bergstrom's boat keeps going, racing toward the island. Waves rise up over the prow and submerge it entirely before lifting and slamming it back down on the rocks. I don't have to do anything else. The boat scrapes against the reef as the current pulls it back again, dropping it in a trough between the waves. The masts seem to reach desperately for the sky, and then the stern disappears completely, dragged down by the weight of the nets. For a second, the bow tilts straight up in the air, and a figure is visible inside the wheelhouse. Then another wave crashes down and the boat is gone.

The clouds are still dark and low when the outline of Jason's boat appears on the horizon. I can't stop him from coming, and I can't stop the storm, but I can try to lure him someplace safe. Safer, at least, than here.

A few yards away, in a calmer part of the inlet, there's a boulder, like a giant cauldron. I wade back into the cold black water and swim out to it just as I start to hear him whispering in my mind. Between the wind, the rain, and the claps of thunder, Jason's thoughts, all of his hopes and wishes, the things he fears, and the things he loves, surround me. It's so easy now. All I have to do is shut my eyes and listen.

"I saw him follow you," Jason says. "And I saw the boat sink." The sun is just starting to peek through the clouds, and he's sitting on the deck of his boat, squinting in the glare from the water.

I'm sitting next to him, wringing water from my hair and peeling off my soaking wet snail stockings. "He came to my house."

Jason starts playing with the zipper on his backpack. "I thought he might. That's why I didn't want you to be alone there."

I run my tongue over my teeth, tasting blood

from where I bit my lip when the gun hit me in the face. "You were right."

"And then you did it to me too? Tricked me, sort of."

"I had no choice. That's what I tried to tell you. When she calls for us, it's like . . . it's impossible to control." I glance at him, waiting for him to say something more, but he's pulled his hood up and tightened the strings, so I can't see his face. "You brought the crown, right?"

He nods and pushes the backpack toward me. "I even wrapped everything in plastic, so it would be waterproof."

"What's wrong? Do you feel sick?"

"No, I'm just— It's different watching you actually do it."

I feel the boat moving up and down in the waves, and suddenly I'm the one who's seasick. "What's different?"

"Nothing." He gets back up and leans over the railing. We're not very far out at sea here, but there's a fog surrounding the island, and it's hard to see the shore. "I guess I just didn't expect it to feel like this."

The sunlight burns my eyes and makes the water seem fractured and confusing. I pull my legs up to my chest and rest my forehead on my knees.

Jason kicks at a coil of rope on the deck, and I think about what really happened four years ago at Lily's first big sleepover party, the night he let her and her friends give him a haircut. I watched the whole thing unfold from a shelf in the linen closet, one I'd recently discovered I could climb into. At first he was okay with the haircut, going along with everything, assuring everyone it was no big deal. He was okay when they brought out one of Dad's old razors and announced they were going to shave his head. And he still seemed okay a few minutes later when they lost interest in the whole operation and ditched him to go make prank phone calls.

But then Jason caught sight of himself in the mirror. And then he started crying. And then he kicked the wall so hard he left a dent.

I didn't ditch Jason to go make prank phone calls that night. When the other girls left, I climbed down from my shelf and told him everything was going to be okay. I helped him sweep up the plaster and the fallen hair and move the garbage can to cover the dent. I made him an ice pack for his swollen foot, and we spent the rest of the night in a fort he made using blankets and the dining room table. I don't remember where our parents were at the time. I don't remember who finally fixed his hair or if anybody ever took him to the doctor for his foot. It's highly possible that nobody ever even noticed. But that was the night it became unofficially official that even though he was Lily's same age, and even though our families were always all together, Jason was my real friend. My first one besides my sisters.

I lift my head. "I guess it's easy being friends with a siren, until you actually get lured someplace."

He sighs. "It's harder than you think."

"Well, if I'm so hard to deal with, then maybe you should just stay here by yourself."

He doesn't say anything else, so I clamber up the side of the boat and throw myself over with the crown still under my arm, letting the freezing sting of saltwater flood my eyes and nose. I come back to the surface, treading water, and Jason yells down to me.

"You forgot your shoes!"

It's a statement of fact, but it feels like the ultimate insult.

I start swimming back to the island. I tell myself that I don't care if he comes along or not. I don't care if he stops being my friend and never speaks to me again. But a few moments later, I hear a splash, and I know it's him swimming along behind.

He follows me up out of the water and onto the black sand beach, and I watch him out of the corner of my eye. Hands braced on his knees and head down, he's struggling to breathe. I've never wanted to hug him and throw something at him at the same time so badly before. Instead, I reach out and grab his hand, just for a second, and I squeeze his fingers, the way I used to during rainstorms, when the wind sounded strong enough to rip right through his mom's trailer and send us all off into outer space, and Alice would tell us to count the miles between the claps of thunder.

"I brought your shoes," he says, and bends to open his backpack. "I was all out of plastic wrap, though, so they're kind of wet."

"Thank you."

I slip the wet shoes on because it's better than being barefoot on the rocks, and I stare down at our feet.

"We'd better get going."

"Wait, Jason. What was it like?"

He picks up a rock and starts examining it, holding it up in the sunlight so flecks of mica glisten and change color. When we were little, he used to collect rocks like that. Pretend they were valuable.

"What was what like?"

"My sisters say that sailors are in a trance the whole time, that afterward, if they live, they don't remember anything at all."

"I guess so." He's still pretending to study the rock, turning it over in his hand like it's the geological discovery of the century. "Yeah, I don't remember. It's like it never even happened."

I nod. "That's what I figured."

"But I would have found you anyway, Lolly. I mean, even if you didn't call for me. I think I still would have found you."

The water is rising, the tide coming in, and

suddenly the broken, rust-splattered body of Mr.
Bergstrom's boat, all scarred and torn apart,
comes rushing out of the sea. It shoots forward,
carving a few feet into the sand, and then tilts on
its side. The masts are gone, and the jagged holes
in the bottom are big enough to see through.

Jason whispers, "Do you think he's still in
there?"

"I don't know."

The damaged boat lies quietly like a beached
whale. There's not a sound anywhere now except
the tide and the seabirds that have begun to circle
closer.

"I've never seen a dead person before, Lolly."

"Me either."

Jason wipes his sleeve across his forehead, and
then he takes the crown from me and puts it on his
head. It's a little big on him, but it doesn't fall off
or anything. It sort of fits. "I'm going to look."

"Do you want me to come with you?"

"No," he says. "Just wait here."

He crosses the beach with a sort of grim
determination and starts climbing up into the
boat. Maybe it's just the crown he's wearing, but

he seems to have gotten taller over the last week. Like, from the back, you might think he was in high school or something.

A few seconds later, he reappears and lowers himself onto the shore.

"What happened?"

He shakes his head. "Let's go."

"Did you see anything?"

Jason pulls the crown off his head and snatches at a tree limb, snapping it down and holding it out in front of him as he starts hacking into the overgrown brush. "No," he says. "There was nobody there."

We start hiking up a barely worn dirt path toward the ruins of Fort O'Malley, tripping over rocks and tree limbs and squelching in our wet shoes. At certain points the trail turns steep, and we have to pull ourselves up, using the gnarled tree roots that stick out of rocks. At first, we don't hear anything but the waves and the birds and the sound of our own footsteps. But soon there's another sound too. A groaning, grumbling, prehistoric sound, and we see them coming out of the woods. Two of them. They have broad, flat heads

and curious brown eyes, and they lumber toward
us on massive paws, sniffing and growling and
pawing at the ground. And then more bears
appear at the edge of the forest, rising up out of
what seemed like empty woods. Each one is bigger
than the last, and I realize that they've been there
the entire time. They have claws like daggers and
moss growing on their fur, and I think they must
be hundreds of years old.

Jason stops and looks at me. "The Kermode.
You see how their fur is almost white?"

I wrap my arms around the crown. "Are they
dangerous?"

"I don't think so. They're like black bears.
Besides, most of these isolated island species don't
have any experience with humans. They don't even
know they're supposed to be afraid."

The bears are still looking at us, little groups
and families of them, some resting on the ground,
some perched on logs, and some sitting in trees,
and we continue up the path, picking our way
carefully over rocks and fallen branches. The
bears turn to watch us pass, and sometimes they
throw their heads back and roar up at the sky, as if

they're seeking some explanation as to what we're doing there. But they don't ever come any closer.

At last, just before sunset, we find ourselves standing in a forest of dwarf pine trees, all bent permanently in the same direction. The sky is burning magenta, and before us lies the steep fall of the canyon. A hawk circles overhead, and we can hear the unnerving sound of the bears bellowing in the distance.

Only one wall of the fort remains. There are archways carved in stone, rusted metal gates bolted to the sides, and one lonesome cannon, riddled with holes.

"It's still standing," Jason says, and runs his hand over one of the walls. The archways are all uneven and crumbling in places, and it looks like that might not be the case for much longer. He looks up at it, amazed. "Can you believe it? My ancestors, my actual biological family, built this with their own hands to protect their land and defend themselves from intruders."

I'm not exactly sure how I feel about forts, and Jason's ancestors, and defending land that may or may not have been theirs to defend in the first

place, but I can see what it means to him. It's significant, like the Sea Witch said, and I bet he wishes he'd
had a fort like this to defend him and his mom when
Mr. Bergstrom first showed up in their lives. "So
where are we going to bury the crown?"

He walks to a place where the wall casts a
rounded shadow in the dirt. "Here," he says.
"This is the right spot. I can feel it. Can't you?"

"Sure," I tell him. "That seems right."

Jason takes two trowels out of his backpack, and
we start to dig. The soil is soft and rich here, not
like the dry, sandy soil at home, and it falls away
easily. Soon we have a good-size hole, and we drop
the crown down inside. It lands with a satisfying
thump. And then we start kicking dirt back in,
until it's all filled up and we can't see the glint of
the crown anymore.

I look at him. "Do you feel anything yet?"

He shrugs. "Do you want a snack?"

"A snack?"

"Yeah." He pulls a thermos and a plastic bag
out of his backpack. He opens the bag and hands
me the thermos. "I brought water and some of
those cookies you hid in my room. They have a

lot of sugar, and I figured that might help with the spell. I mean, I think it's important to be prepared."

I take a sip of water and wipe my mouth with the back of my hand. "I'm prepared."

"I wasn't saying you weren't."

"Well, I'm just saying I am."

"You actually have no supplies with you at all."

"I had a bag," I tell him. I decide not to mention that it was mainly filled with library books and sea glass. "Besides, I'm prepared in other ways."

He opens a package of cookies and hands it to me, and I give him back the thermos. He takes a drink from it.

"You know that's full of germs now, right?" I say.

"I'm not scared of germs anymore," he informs me, as if it's a thing that happened three years ago instead of last week.

"Oh," I tell him. "Well, good."

One of the spirit bears has followed us all the way up from the beach, and now it's standing on a rock nearby, watching. Every time I turn around, it tilts its milky-white head to one side, and we look at each other. And for some reason, I remember something Jason once told me, about why he's so fascinated by marine biology. He said it's that you see all these bizarre, impossible-seeming creatures, these fish with lanterns attached to their heads, and vampire squids, and sea snails with wings, and they all seem totally weird—but then you learn the science behind them, you get to understand where they came from and how they work, and you realize that they actually make perfect sense. In fact, you realize they never could have been any other way.

After we eat, I sit cross-legged in the dirt where we buried the crown and straighten my back because I feel like receiving a spell calls for good posture. Jason sits down in front of me and rubs his finger in the dirt, and then he traces a crescent shape on my forehead the way the Sea Witch showed us.

"Do you remember how it goes?" I ask.

"Of course I remember how it goes."

"I'm just checking."

"Lolly, I wouldn't forget the spell at a time like this."

He draws the crescent shape again and clears his throat—pausing, I think, to make sure I don't interrupt again. Then he repeats the words exactly the way the Sea Witch did, even getting the accent and the intonation right.

And then we wait.

For a while we just sit there and nothing happens. The spirit bears go about their business, and the hawks call to one another, and the sky turns a deep navy blue. The shadows grow long and cold.

"How are we supposed to know if it worked?" Jason asks.

"I have no idea," I tell him.

"Does anything seem different to you?"

"Everything seems different."

He nods. "I guess that's how we know."

On the way back home, Jason stands at the helm of his sailboat and I sit on the deck wrapped in his jacket and gloves, even though I'm pretty sure it'll be a long time before I ever feel anything like warm again.

After a few minutes, he comes and lies down next to me. "You see the fireworks?" He points out across the harbor. "We're almost home."

Sure enough, we can see the lights of Starbridge

Cove from here, and the fireworks from the festival. We lie on our backs and watch them for a little while. As they do each year, the fireworks become increasingly complex as the show goes on, until suddenly there are a million crackling explosions going off over our heads at once, illuminating the entire sky and turning everything green and gold, and it feels as if we've fallen into some other dimension. Jason looks like an alien, and the sails billowing over our heads seem like ghosts.

But then it's over. The fireworks leave trails of ash shaped like jellyfish, and the night is black again and filled with stars. The sails are not haunted, and we're back to just being ourselves.

"I think that was the finale," I tell him.

"You know what you asked me about before, Lolly?" he says. "About what it felt like when you called?"

"Yeah?"

"I lied. I do remember. I just couldn't think how to say it."

I prop myself up on my elbows. "Can you think of it now?"

"Yeah," he says. "It felt like not being alone."

Chapter
7

Sweet sad songs sung by lonely girls
—*Lucinda Williams*

Late that night, Jason and I come ashore and walk to the motel. We see the neon sign first, flickering in the distance, and then the hospital-bright lights of the lobby. And then we see them, all the faded, sleepy sirens with their hollow eyes and messy hair, stumbling out into the darkness. Dozens of them. They're drinking diet sodas from the vending machine, lighting cigarettes, and stealing getaway cars from the parking lot. So many that at first, we can't find my sisters.

We push our way inside the lobby, where this

awful canned music is playing and the vending machine looks like it exploded. "There!" Jason recognizes Lula, sitting on the front desk. She's wearing one of the hotel towels and trying to open a bag of pretzels with her teeth.

When she sees us, Lula jumps down from the counter and throws her arms around my neck. "Lolly, do you know what's going on? How did we get here?"

Lara and Lily are coming down the stairs, pushed and jostled in the sea of ghost girls streaming toward the exit, but when they see us, they drift closer, and the four of us become a tangle of arms and legs, with everyone hugging and talking at once.

I slip Lara's necklace off and press it into her hand. "I found this."

She smiles and touches my forehead. "Where have you been, Lolly? You look so different."

Lula shovels a handful of pretzels in her mouth. "We're starving."

"Why is it so cold in here?" Lily asks. "Who are all these people?" One of the other girls, weaving a groggy path through the crowd, bumps right into her. "Ow!" Lily calls out. "Watch it."

The girl doesn't respond. She takes a few more steps and then pauses by the front door, blocking it. Her lips are moving, and I watch her for a second, trying to figure out what she's saying. Her eyes are ice blue, nearly colorless, and her feet are swollen to twice their normal size, covered in thick, gray scales and fringed by nails like claws. She's all wrapped up in a white bathrobe with the motel logo stitched on it and the belt looped twice around her waist, and she's staring up at the loud-speaker like it's the strangest thing she's ever seen. Or maybe it's the opposite. Maybe it's the only thing in the room that makes any sense.

Jason leans over and whispers, "What's wrong with her?"

"She's blind," I tell him. I look from one girl to the next, at the way they hold on to one another and grip the walls. "All of these girls are. They can't see."

The blind girl starts singing then, harmoniz-ing, taking that irritating little melody and making it sound full and rich with her voice. She plays with each note the way seabirds toss tiny fish in the air before they swallow them. And the other girls, who were lining up behind her like lobsters in a trap, pushing and climbing over each other to get out—they stop when they hear her voice. And then they start singing too, automatically, like a reflex. One and then another and another, like birds on a telephone wire.

Two nights ago, in the darkness of the motel room, I thought these girls looked a lot like us. But I was wrong. These girls are not like us. These girls are not even remotely human. And their voices, no matter how perfect, are nothing but sad and useless, dulled by the pain of manipulating and pretending and the fact that nobody who matters will ever hear them. Dulled by whatever sacrifice it was that brought them here in the first place and kept them alive like this for way too long.

It's not worth it, I think. *It's not worth it to live like one of these blind zombie bird girls.*

I link my arm through Lara's and start pulling her toward the door. "Come on," I say. "Let's get out of here."

On the walk back to our house, I watch my sisters in the passing headlights, moving single file down the side of the road, and I think about what the Sea Witch told me, about the sacrifice they made. I keep thinking about it all night, even after we get home and begin cleaning up the broken glass and putting the living room in order. All this time, I thought my sisters chose to become sirens because they wanted to be beautiful and powerful and immortal. But that's not what happened at all. They did it for me. When I died, they were right there in the grave-yard with a flashlight, and a shovel, and a spell from the Sea Witch. They were willing to trade their own lives just to bring me back.

Later, I follow Lara into the kitchen to help make hot chocolate. She places a little saucepan on the stove and pours milk into it. "You want the yellow seashell mug, Lolly?"

I nod. "Sure." She knows it's my favorite.

"Okay. Get the chili pepper." That's her secret ingredient.

I take the container from the spice rack and hand it to her. Then I hop up on the counter and grab a wooden spoon to help stir the milk. She glances at me. "Don't bang your feet on the cabinets."

"Lara?"

"Yes?"

"Thank you."

"For what?"

"For everything."

She reaches out and pulls on my ponytail. "You're welcome, little one."

The next morning, a headline appears in the local paper:

LANDOWNER, ERIK BERGSTROM, AMONG CASUALTIES OF LAST NIGHT'S STORM

Jason's mom and stepbrothers get dressed up in suits and drive down to Portland to speak with an attorney, and Jason gets to stay home alone. The first thing he does is take all the stuffed animal heads down from the walls and shut off the air-conditioning. Then he and I sit upstairs in the nook by the picture window with my history textbook and Hannah's diary and we read every word.

March 2nd, 1710

Several weeks ago, one of the orphan girls from the village knocked at my door and begged me to cure her sister of a fever. Every night now, I have them

*both out there by the water, luring the hateful ships
to our shore, searching for Rebecca.*

We read about the centuries of lost, orphan girls who worked for the Sea Witch, girls like my sisters and me, and how some of them ended up running away, and some were hypnotized and kidnapped, and some just vanished and were never heard from again. Nobody ever succeeded in undoing the spell, though. None of them could ever figure out how.

*Abigail says she's finished being a seiren. She is in
love with one of the boys in our village and wants to
be married. But I will not let her go. Not yet.
When Rebecca comes home safely, then, perhaps,
I will recite this spell for forgiveness and reunite
the broken pieces of my soul. Then, perhaps, I will
find peace. And then I will set them all free.*

"What are the broken pieces of her soul?" Jason asks.

"Maybe it's the wolf," I tell him. "She wrote in one of the earlier entries that the wolf appeared in her jail cell on the night the judge sentenced her to hang. I think she took all of the anger and terror she felt that night and used it to conjure him. He's her protector now. And the rest of her soul, her real self, is hidden away somewhere in the ocean. That's how she has the ability to cast these spells, to do this kind of magic. That's what makes her a sea witch."

"But how do we get the wolf away from her?"

"I don't think it's enough to take him away. It's not like Mr. Bergstrom and his crown. Her power doesn't come from the wolf; it comes from being broken into pieces, from hiding the soft ones away and keeping the tough ones close. Now, if we could put all of her pieces back together, if we could summon the wolf ourselves and reunite him with her soul, we could probably undo all of the spells she's ever cast. We could help her find peace and set the rest of us free."

"But maybe she doesn't want to find peace." Jason sets the book back on the floor. "I mean, we can't change what happened to her. Maybe she just wants to stay mad."

"Look, you have your stepfather's power now.

You have the ability to perform spells, and she gave that to you. She helped you find it. Maybe she wants you to use it. Maybe she's as tired of the shipwrecks as we are. Maybe she just wanted somebody to hear her story and understand. Maybe she just wanted somebody to listen."

"But the ocean is a big place, Lolly. Even if she is ready to move on, and even if we do the spell for forgiveness and it works, how is the wolf supposed to find his way to her soul?"

"I know," I tell him. "I have an idea."

Ms. Cross lives in a little blue house on a side street a few blocks from the diner. Her screen door is shut, but the front door is open, and soft yellow lamplight spills out onto the porch. Jason and I race up the front steps, and Jason rings the bell. A few moments later, a woman in an oversize sweater and slippers comes to the door. She's one of the folksingers from the festival, the one who strolls around town with a painted guitar.

"Hello?" she says.

"We're looking for Ms. Cross," I tell her. "She, um, she lives here, right?"

The woman smiles. "Yes," she says. "Are you students of hers?"

"Yes." Jason holds out his hand. "Jason O'Malley."

They shake hands, and I'm impressed again at his ability to transform into a grown-up at exactly the right moment.

"Addie," the woman says. "Just a second." She walks back into the hall and calls up the stairs. "Julia! You have visitors."

I don't like the thought of Ms. Cross having a first name, let alone family members who call her by it, but I know somehow that's just a sign of me not being quite as grown-up as Jason, so I try to push it from my mind.

Ms. Cross comes down the stairs and steps out onto the porch. She's also wearing slippers, and it's the first time I've ever seen her without her waterproof boots. "Well, hello," she says. "It's very nice to see you two, but I'm afraid it's almost dinnertime. Can this wait until normal business hours?"

"No," I tell her. "We have something for you. Like, an offer."

"It's important," Jason clarifies. "Otherwise, we wouldn't impose."

Impose? I think.

"Well, then." She pushes her glasses up on her nose and grabs a shawl from the coatrack. "We'd better have a seat."

Ms. Cross turns on the porch light, and we sit together on the front steps, balancing the diary and the textbook across our laps in the gathering darkness.

"You were right," I tell her. "I know the author of this diary, and she is in trouble."

"What do you mean you know her? Lorelei, this diary is hundreds of years old."

"Yes, but she's still alive. She's been alive this entire time, and she still lives here, on an island not far from town."

"She's not quite human," Jason explains. "She's become sort of a . . . well, I hate to use the term now, but"—he lowers his voice—"a *witch*."

I look up at Ms. Cross. "And your family was involved in the trials, right? They were witnesses during the trial of Hannah Martin."

"Yes." Ms. Cross laces her fingers together. "In

fact, that is one of the great sadnesses of my life, knowing how they behaved. What they did to her."

"Well, you were right that the author of this diary is her. It's Hannah Martin. But the thing is, she's still alive, and she's still in pain. And there's a chance now for you to help her."

Down the block, streetlights start to flicker on, and one of the neighbors comes out through his garage carrying a garbage can. He waves to us, and Ms. Cross takes off her glasses and waves back. "Hello, Mr. Hale!" She dabs at the corner of her eye with her sleeve. "Even if that were true," she whispers, "what could I possibly do about it now? It's been three hundred years."

"You could apologize."

"What?"

"It's not too late," Jason says. "Three hundred years is nothing. I mean, not when you really think about it."

"Well." She smiles a little. "I suppose that's true."

"You could write her an apology."

"Please," I say. "Even if it wasn't your fault, you understand what she went through. And you're sorry about it. Like, really truly sorry about what happened. It would help her to know that. I know it would."

"And it would help Lolly," Jason says. "And her sisters. And a bunch of other girls too. You could keep them from being a part of this cycle. You could help make them human again."

"You know who they are," I say. "The other ones. You've been worried about them this whole time. You told me. Please. Just acknowledge what happened and tell her you're sorry. Otherwise, all of this—the storms, and the shipwrecks, and the kidnapped girls—it's all going to get worse."

Ms. Cross is quiet for a moment, looking down at her feet, and the wind keeps lifting the fringes of her shawl. "Yes," she says, and it's almost like she's speaking to herself. "I believe that would be the right thing to do. In fact, it is the only thing. Apologize. How else is one to proceed?" She shuts the diary and gets to her feet. "All right, children," she says. "I'll write the letter. Come inside."

"There's one last thing," I tell her.

"Yes?"

"We need to borrow the lanterns from your classroom. All of them."

"Actually," Jason says, "we'd like to keep them."

The next morning, all of us are scheduled to work at the diner. I sit at my usual perch by the entrance, and I watch as my sisters glide back and forth, trays held gracefully aloft, balancing juice and coffees and slices of pie. Lara slips past me and winks. "Almost time to start your server training, Lolly." I smile back at her, but I don't say anything. I can't. I wait until she walks away, and then I take a tube of her lipstick out of my pocket, the same one Lula used to draw on my hand, and I draw a tiny heart on the side of the seating chart. Another symbol. This time it's for them, so they'll know not to be afraid.

Lula's brewing a fresh pot of coffee, and Lily's carrying a tray of apple crumb to the display case. It's just a normal day, but I sit and watch everything for a few minutes, trying to breathe in all the sweetness like steam from one of Lara's hot chocolates.

It's not too busy, but most of our regular

customers are there. Coach Bouchard's motor-cycle is in the parking lot, and he and Nurse Claire are having lunch together, holding hands across the table and sharing a piece of lemon meringue. The gymnastics girls are all packed into the big table in back, eating ice cream sundaes and wear-ing matching track suits. Addie and Ms. Cross are sitting together in a booth in the corner with pan-cakes and a crossword puzzle.

The last thing I do is make two sandwiches and pack them up in "to go" boxes. Dad's not home yet, and I'm not supposed to use the stove by myself, so I make myself tuna fish on whole wheat, and peanut butter with strawberry jelly for Jason, so he won't have to deal with any mayonnaise. Then I wait by the door.

Finally, Dad's rusty blue hatchback, the car he's been driving since he left us his truck, turns the corner and pulls around to the employee parking lot. I grab the sandwiches and my jacket and hat and go out back to meet him. It's a cold, clear morning with bright winter light glinting off every surface, and Dad's bent over, taking suitcases out of the trunk. He looks tired and pale; his shoulders are slumped and there are dark circles under his eyes.

"Welcome back," I tell him, and point to the sandwiches. "I'm leaving early."

He turns around and smiles. "Nice to see you too, kid."

"Did you have a good time?"

He runs his hands through his hair and shrugs. "I guess so. Yeah, I did. What about you? How's it feel being thirteen? You feel any older?"

"I guess so."

"So where are you running off to?"

"To Jason's. It's because we have to work on a project together. I mean, it's for school."

"Sure, kid. Whatever you need."

I put the sandwiches down and push my hands into my pockets. "There's something else, too."

"Okay."

"Can you put down the guitar?"

"Sure." Dad puts down his guitar case. He takes a seat on one of his suitcases and starts playing with the handle. In his oversize jacket, he kind of looks like a kid who just got sent to detention. "What is it?"

"We need you to stop living at the diner and move back home. To our house. I know Lara's technically an adult, and Lula's sixteen, but still. It's not the same. You're a good dad, okay? At least, you're good enough. And we need you."

Dad doesn't say anything for a while. He just keeps sitting there on that suitcase. And the longer I look, the more he starts to seem like the vulnerable one, the one so lost he couldn't find his way back now if he tried. "I'm no good in that house, Lolly. I can't ever seem to fall asleep there anymore. Even here, I usually just stay up late playing music. I guess I don't sleep very well anywhere these days."

"That's okay," I tell him. "None of us do."

"Well, it's not that simple." He curls his fingers around the handle. "What if I lose her again?"

"Who?"

"Your mother. I mean, I can find her so easily now. When I walk into that house, it's like no time passed at all. Every room, every piece of furniture— it's all memories of her. I like it that way. I want to keep it that way. So, what if I move back home and it stops feeling like that? What if I move back and life just goes on and then I can't find her anymore?"

"Dad—" I can't bring myself to say what I'm thinking. *She's already gone.*

He takes one of my gloved hands and threads our fingers together. "I guess I never thought of staying away as leaving you. I thought of it more as holding on to her."

For some reason, I start thinking about that grief pamphlet I got from Nurse Claire. And I think about Hannah and Rebecca and all the things people try to hold on to and can't. And all the things they end up wrecking when they try.

"Well, listen," Dad says. "I'm gonna get myself a cup of coffee. Can I get you one too?"

"Okay."

"And you want to split some fries with your old man? I'll make 'em right now."

"Yeah, Dad. Sounds good."

"Great." He stands and touches my forehead, the purple bruise flowering around my eye. He has no idea what happened to me and, as usual, he doesn't ask. But a look of concern flickers across his face. "I'm sorry you're hurt, Lolly. None of this is your fault, okay? I mean, you know that, right?"

I nod. "I know."

"Look, your mother and I weren't always the best parents. That's why we had so many of you. So you'd take care of each other."

"That's not even funny."

He squeezes my shoulder. "I'll be right back with the fries, kid. We can eat out here. It's not too cold, right?"

"No, it's fine."

And I guess it is.

Sometimes I wish I could tell Dad everything. I wish he wasn't always so lost in his own head, and that he could understand my sisters and me and what's happened to us. But I guess something that happens when you grow up in a restaurant is you learn to accept what's available. Usually it's best not to push too hard for things that aren't on the menu.

Without thinking too much more about it, I pick up my sandwiches and walk out to the road. I leave before he comes back.

At sunset, Jason and I walk to the sound, which is a quiet body of water, between the cliffs, that feeds into the sea. We're carrying our sandwiches, Ms. Cross's apology, Hannah's diary, a pack of matches, and a box containing all of the lanterns from my classroom. Jason is wearing one of Mr. Bergstrom's old Viking helmets. He says he thinks it might help us with the spell, but I think he just likes wearing it. At night now, he sleeps with it under his bed.

Together, we kneel on the shore and unfold the paper with Ms. Cross's apology. The sun is vanishing slowly, shimmering in the trees, and we open Hannah's diary and recite the spell that's written there, the spell for forgiveness. Then Jason strikes a match and burns the apology, sending sparks and ashes up into the air. And then we set to work lighting the lanterns. Jason arranges them in an evenly spaced pattern, and I follow along behind with the matches and light each one.

Jason looks at me. "Are you okay?"

"I think so."

"You know, I'm still not sure I believe everything the Sea Witch—I mean, Hannah—I'm not sure if I believe everything she told us. But if it's true what she said about the night your mom died, about giving your sisters a spell to bring you back from the dead, and if we're about to undo all of her spells, then that might mean—"

"It's the only way," I tell him. "Otherwise my sisters and I will end up like the girls in the motel, and I don't want that. They saved me, and now I want to save them."

"Well, take this." Jason digs in his pocket for a second and draws out some rope.

"What is it?"

"It's a bracelet I made from one of my sailor's knots. It's supposed to keep you safe, like during storms and stuff."

I hold out my arm, and he ties the bracelet around my wrist.

"Thank you."

"If it is true," he says, "what Hannah said, and if this works, I don't—I don't know what I'm going to do without you."

I think about that for a long time. I want to tell him that I'll always be with him. That he doesn't have to worry because we'll be together, forever, no matter what. But then, that sounds suspiciously like something a siren would say. Because sirens

don't tell you the truth. Sirens only tell you what
you want to hear.

Instead, I pick up the first lantern and place it
in the water. He follows me, and, one by one, we
set them all to sail. "Are you scared?" he asks.

I shake my head. "Not anymore."

A strange warm breeze gusts by, and the lanterns start to slip away from the shore. Bobbing
gently in the current, each presses lightly against
the one ahead of it, and we hold hands and watch
as they drift together, flickering, into the unknown.

Acknowledgments

I am incredibly lucky to have had the support of the following people in creating this book:

Alex Slater, who found this story, understood it completely, and made it shine

Fiona Simpson, who cared for these characters and gave them a wonderful home at Aladdin/Simon & Schuster

Jessica Handelman, who designed the beautiful cover

Eva and Miriam, who read early drafts

Renee, Rachel, Ellen, and Mia, who astound me with their strength, beauty, and humor

Mort, brave champion of the quirky, imaginative, and risk-taking among us

Liana, Tara, Halley, Kristina, Maggie, Natalie, Jamie, Ankur, and Sean, with whom I shared the million grilled cheese sandwiches and late-night diners of adolescence

Laura, who makes it fun to come to work and who makes "little lady" sound cool

The families, teachers, staff, and administrators of Rockland Country Day School

Vashti, who took such good care of Mia

The Samuelson family, who have been so welcoming and supportive

Phil, who believed it was possible long before I did

Paul, who changed our lives

I would also like to acknowledge the work of the Maine-Wabanaki Truth and Reconciliation Commission, whose report about inequalities in the child welfare system inspired portions of this story (learn more about their work here: http://digitalcommons .bowdoin.edu/maine-wabanaki-trc/)

About the Author

DANA LANGER is a high school teacher and the author of *Siren Sisters*. She holds a BA in creative writing and an MA in teaching from Brandeis University where she received the Dafna Zamarripa-Gesundheit Fiction Prize. Dana currently lives in New York City with her husband and daughter. You can visit her online at dana-langer.com and follow her on Twitter at @danicalanger.